I0598934

A STUDY IN CRIMSON

Or, The Tale of the Red Man

WILL BRANDON

SPUR, TEXAS
boldfacebooks.com

Boldface Books trade paperback edition, November 2023
Printed in the United States of America
ISBN 978-1-935619-54-3

1 2 3 4 5   27 26 25 24 23

This book was set in the Birch and Farmhand display and (naturally)
Baskerville body faces in Adobe InDesign 2022 for the Macintosh computer.

Cover and interior design by The Paragraph Ranch

Thanks go to the Crew of the Barque Lone Star, Dallas, Texas,
for permission to reprint portions previously published in their
annual anthologies.

WWW.BOLDFACEBOOKS.COM • WWW.BOOKADELPHIA.COM

Praise for Will Brandon's *THE WOLF HUNT*

THE WOLF HUNT runs at the head of the pack as a great read.
– MIKE COX, author of *Gunsights and Sites in Texas Ranger History*

An amazing blend of mystery mixed with Western culture.
Drama and action compel the reader to turn the pages until the final
satisfying end. —HISTORICAL NOVELS REVIEW

When reverence for classic literature combines with excellent writing
and a knack for atmospheric description, the inevitable result is great
reading. Holmes and Watson themselves would approve–
and so will you. — JEFF GUINN, 2018 Western Writers of
America Spur Award winner for Best Traditional Novel

With The Wolf Hunt, *Will Brandon brings fresh characters*
and a new landscape to a beloved genre. I hope that Capt.
Derrick Miles's Houston Street office address becomes as famous
as Sherlock Holmes's 221B Baker Street. —HENRY CHAPPELL,
author of *Silent We Stood,* 2014 winner of the Western Writers of
America Spur Award for best historical novel

In this strikingly original mystery, a detective very, very much in the
Sherlock Holmes mold works suavely through the clues of
an eerie apparent murder.
— DONALD MACE WILLIAMS,
author of *Wolfe and Other Poems*

A terrific reimagining of a classic tale . . . Brandon captures the
rugged beauty of the Caprock country the way Wyman Meinzer
captures it in photography. –MILES ARCENEAUX, author of
Thin Slice of Life and other Gulf Coast mystery novels

A Study in Crimson,
or, The Tale of the Red Man

FORT WORTH, TEXAS, LOOKING SOUTH FROM THE TRINITY RIVER
DRAWN BY D. D MORSE, APRIL 1876

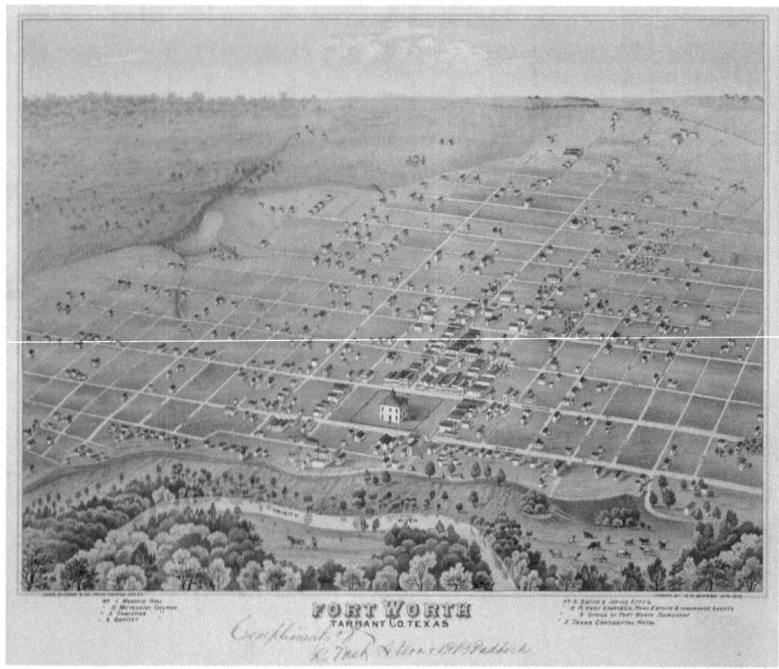

I COUGHED MY WAY THROUGH TEN MORE BLOCKS *of dust and haze as I trod up Main, almost to the river, before realizing that Houston Street must run parallel to my path on the west. Lot of good my Army orienteering course was doing me here in this godforsaken cowtown. If I was to make any sort of success here I'd certainly need a map.* —PAGE 48

Contents

BONUS CONTENT BEGINS ON PAGE 121

Part I

{Being an extract from the journal of
FRANKLIN C. HOOPER, M.D., A.F.&A.M.}

Chapter 1

CAPTAIN DERRICK MILES

{In which a meeting takes place in the Panther City.}

HOW I, SCION OF AN OLD GALVESTON FAMILY and a Philadelphia-trained physician, came to be stationed beside the malodorous marge of Sycamore Creek east of the rough-and-ready town of Fort Worth, Texas, in the rising heat of a midsummer morning, with nothing in my possession but valise, medical bag, and camera kit is something of a long story, and one I shall in due time relate.

But I will say forthwith that such a position placed me in the path of fate, not only as I proved to have chosen the perfect spot for an historic photograph, but that I experienced, in that inscrutable way that the trio of weaving goddesses has ascribed to each man his individual destiny before ever he utters his first syllable or rises on his own toddling toes, the twist of the skein that changed my life forever.

That is to say, it placed me in the path of Mr. Derrick Miles.

Purely out of curiosity I had hired a buggy to drive me out from Dallas to the Eagle Ford camp. I'd arrived in the city only the day before, weary and unwashed, heartsick and chastened after a hasty and ignominious departure from my coastal hometown.

But I had read the papers on the train, of course. The drama had been building for weeks and days. The Texas & Pacific was pushing to beat a deadline. If it did not complete its contracted route into the city of Fort Worth by noon on the nineteenth of July, 1876, the railroad would forfeit all of its lucrative government incentives. It was said that bets were being laid on either outcome as swiftly as miles of track.

How could a man with time on his hands and an expensive photographic setup resist attempting to record such a moment? Upon reaching Dallas the prior evening, after a journey of three days, I'd treated myself to a bathe, a shave, a decent meal, and a good night's sleep at the Fairmont, and rose early.

My hack departed right after breakfast and followed the T&P right-of-way for seven and a half miles along well-trodden road, in considerable company. Onlookers had apparently come out daily to follow the railroad's frenzied westward progress. Upon reaching the creek bank, where a bright red locomotive and tender pulling a single car had halted while track was being extended before our very eyes, I stepped down into the gray soil, mindful as much as possible of my freshly shined boots.

Crowds on the opposite bank outnumbered even those on the Eagle Ford side. I saw to my dismay that I would have to be satisfied with the view from there on the east bank of the reedy stream, since there was no simple way for an ordinary spectator to traverse it and be standing within the city limits as the business end of the locomotive arrived. A series of sleepers from the Fort Worth side had been extended on wooden piers sunk into the mud without even a proper trestle, and beams and ties were being flung across that foundation with little care for precision.

Shouts of the foremen and heave-hos of the laborers filled the air, punctuated by the clang of sledgehammers in alternating rhythm. The hullaballoo put me in mind of a story I'd read in *Leslie's* a while back about the Union and Pacific converging at Promontory Point, in Utah Territory. The furious energy here on Sycamore Creek could be no less than what had led up to that momentous meeting of May 1869.

About me, parties of men, women, and children had begun to spread blankets upon the ground, or set up campaign tables and folding chairs. Some fifty yards away, on the opposite side, a similar scene was unfolding, with even more abandon. Through the clouds of dust I could make out men with spyglasses trained on the action, and a gaggle of reporters stood or squatted with pencils and pads at the ready. The telegraph wire that had been rigged across a makeshift network of poles hummed.

I set out my wooden tripod and carefully mounted the Scovill box camera on its platform, then ducked underneath the black cloth and maneuvered a plate from my pack into the slot. I would have to be judicious in choosing the right moment, I realized, as I had brought only three prepared plates with me, and without a darkroom in the field I would have to guess at the exposure time. I could only hope experience would supplement luck today.

I focused the lens on the mighty engine that stood still but boilers ready, its funnel disgorging white clouds against a vivid blue sky, though I knew that contrast would be lost in the final image. The blue-sensitive chemicals would also render the engine's paint scheme in deep black.

Through the finding lens I saw the steam clouds build and billow, and I heard a quick blast on the whistle. A commotion grew around the locomotive, and I withdrew from under the stifling cloth momentarily to see what had piqued the crowd's interest. Workmen from the near side of the creek were heaving an enormous timber into place across the remaining piers to span the gap, making way for bolts to be driven in and iron rail to be laid down upon it. The engine seemed to strain at its blocks with pent-up power, as a thoroughbred might press the gate before the starting gun of a five-furlong race.

I gazed into the lens again and awaited my moment. Figures moved in and out of the foreground obscured by drifts of steam, when suddenly I spied a most curious sight. Among the throngs a tallish man with beaked nose and ruddy complexion, in dark braids and beaded buckskin shirt, emerged stealthily from the behind the train, crossed the tracks, and slipped into the crowd, coming closer to my direction. But the odd figure was quickly lost among the clusters of hats and parasols, and I wondered if I had not invented him. Such an appearance, I felt, would be provocative indeed in the current climate. Amid the recent animosity toward the red man following the massacre of Custer's troops that had dominated recent headlines, any Indian might well look to his own scalp.

I returned my concentration to the task and refocused the lens, trying to ignore the sweat building on my brow beneath the black cloth. I chose my moment and flipped the lens open. Eighteen seconds, I gauged, holding my breath as my watch ticked away the interval and hoping the locomotive would hold still just – *one* – *more* –

At last, at the end of that eternity, I let the lens cover slip back and exited the cover like a swimmer coming up for air. But I very nearly stumbled over the tripod as I found that tall and exotic figure I had noted earlier standing right over my shoulder and taking a keen interest in my camera setup. He had sneaked up on me in his moccasins. The savage's tousled black braids, intertwined with rawhide and feathers, swung in front of his chest as he leaned in more closely toward the apparatus. A pungent scent emanated from a leather pouch strung around his neck. A soiled fringed bag hung over his shoulder; I hardly had time to observe whether it might contain a weapon.

"Pardon me," the intruder said to me in very un-Indian inflection, "but might you permit me to inspect your outfit?"

With incredulity, and no little amount of alarm, I opened my mouth to inquire why, but had no opportunity to utter any response before the stranger's head and shoulders, folded down almost to nothingness, disappeared beneath the cloth. I was left open-mouthed, searching the crowd for a constable but unwilling to step away from my delicate equipment to seek aid.

No matter, though, for with the same swiftness the intruder had appeared, he emerged from the blind—in an entirely different mien. In that brief moment when I had taken my eyes from the black-draped camera, had a sorcerer's trick been played? For before me stood a gentleman in collared sack coat, shirt and cravat, and a short cap which could have belonged to hunter or soldier; the face which only seconds before had been red appeared now as sallow as a flour biscuit, though sunburned. Gone were the braids and moccasins.

"What the deuce—" I mumbled.

"Sorry, but I must be off," said the man, shouldering his bag and turning toward the tracks. "Fine rig you've got there, by the way."

"Wha—who are you? Where are you going?" I finally managed to spit out.

He looked back at me over the upturned collar of his coat. "Why, to board the train, of course." I caught the slightest glimpse of a lifted eyebrow. "Would you care to capture the image of a lifetime, my man?"

Whether still in the recent grip of some season of impetuosity, or having taken leave of my senses amid the July heat, I do not know, but I found myself for the second time in a single week making a move quite out of character if asked by those who would profess to know me.

I grabbed my gear. "Wait up!" I shouted.

A fierce whistle emanated from the steam engine and a brake released somewhere under its carriage. Stumbling across the impromptu picnic ground among wagons and buggies, I hefted my belongings and tried to keep up with the shape-shifting stranger. Whatever scheme he had in mind, I told myself, it was not too late for me to abandon course.

But a few steps more and there I was, standing beneath the scant shadow of the locomotive as the sun rose higher. The figure I had followed approached the conductor, who was perched on the iron steps at the back of a flatcar, and over the din I caught a few of his words.

"My colleague and I have brought with us the latest in photographic equipment . . . a splendid Scovill view camera with Holmes, Booth & Hayden lens . . . its equal not to be found in all of Texas."

I shouldered my way in closer. The conductor did not look convinced.

The stranger continued. "Now, we are quite aware that General Dodge has photographers waiting just a quarter mile away in the city, ready to document this historic arrival. Given the angle of the sun in their faces, they might or might not succeed in obtaining a proper exposure, though of course they recognize the possibility of total failure. But—" and here the man punctuated his plea with a combination of persuasion and insouci-ance— "if the Texas & Pacific wishes to capture the image of a veritable sea of exuberant future patrons from the unique perspective aboard this train, why, my partner and I stand ready to help it do so."

The conductor glanced my way. I could only nod repeatedly, feeling myself cast in the rôle of foil in a three-penny melodrama.

"Better make it snappy, then," said the conductor, and my leading man hoisted himself up the steps first before giving me a hand and assisting with my baggage.

"Next stop, Pantherville!" shouted the engineer out the window up ahead, as the iron wheels began to roll.

The locomotive's funnel spewed a bituminous cloud on our faces as fire-men slowly built speed. As the train jostled forward I hastened to find an unoccupied spot on the car among crates and tools and timbers to set up the camera. The conductor, duty done for the time being, strode forward to our position just behind the tender.

"Name's Beale," he shouted at us. "Engineer up there's Kelly. He'll be taking it slow this morning. We got some pretty big gaps between the rail sections, but we can make it if he babies her across the creek. Track's not even ballasted yet from here to the end of the line."

I hoped Beale didn't take note of my alarm at his pronouncement.

Instead he continued, "Say, fellas, I didn't get your names."

The stranger spoke before I could pause in my preparations. "My colleague is Doctor Franklin Hooper, a practitioner not only of photography but of medicine," said my new companion, to my further astonishment. "And I'm Derrick Miles, at your service."

Beale chuckled. "That fits. But we won't be makin' many miles today. All's we have to do is cross the city limits. And just between you gents and me and the fencepost, it's a good thing the Fort Worth city fathers slipped in and moved the boundary line this way a few hundred yards, or we might not make that deadline a-tall today."

I concentrated on readying the camera and would save my questions for later, for the big Number 20 locomotive ahead of us had moved out over water—what little there was, but some twenty feet below us down a steep embankment, still—and we inched toward the expectant, cheering faces across the way.

Moments later, at precisely 11:23 a.m. by my vest-pocket watch, a great roar went up, and a shotgun fired off, and a Texas flag was unfurled from a bandstand. This was the scene I'd been waiting for. I clicked the shutter back, held it for twenty long seconds as the train slowed to a creep, and prayed the movement wouldn't blur the image too badly. I would not know the results until I succeeded in locating a laboratory in the city to develop my plates. I did not know which of my efforts had yielded fruit, nor would I until that eventual hour.

Nor did I know that when I stepped off that train it would be onto the soil of my new home and into the start of a new life. And neither did I know that the mystery man who had identified himself as Derrick Miles would figure momentously in it.

The locomotive came to a halt at last where the Texas & Pacific crew had constructed a bulwark several blocks from the town, with its impressive sprawl of commercial establishments, hotels, and houses. We departed the train with some haste—it appeared Miles's intrusion might not have been entirely sanctioned—and promised to deliver photographs to the company on the morrow.

A glance at my companion, however, told me he was in no shape to withstand more time out in the open, at midday. The signs of sunburn on his brow, which may have contributed to my initial impression of a red complexion, seemed to have deepened. Or had I imagined that bizarre scene? It seemed as something out of a distant dream, as did the former life I had left behind me on the far side of Sycamore Creek. Maybe I was the one suffering from heat delirium.

But my new acquaintance Derrick Miles had in certainty begun to sweat more profusely than the warm day might warrant, and I prescribed for both of us a treatment for our thirst. Having not considered the prospect of a mile's journey on foot uphill from the miasmic flats where the train had halted, however, I had no plan for myself, much less an ailing companion, regarding how to reach town.

I looked about. Scores of wheeled conveyances and four-legged beasts of burden seemed to be turning and heading out in a common west-northwest direction, an exodus I presumed to be aiming for the city and its much-touted drinking establishments. They were not waiting for their Moses, the mayor, to lead them.

The platform party, it appeared, had arrived via a chartered omnibus, whose driver was now lounging in the box and allowing his team to graze quietly in the shade while his fares expected to return together at their leisure. Said fares, it seemed, had also come prepared for long speeches and brought libations of their own. After pouring out a necessary thimbleful to the deities of fire and iron, they proceeded to empty a jeroboam of Moët et Chandon into silver goblets on a table next to the bandstand. Attendants were busy setting out wicker baskets of comestibles.

As the city fathers backslapped one another and their ladies looked on, an idea occurred to me, for remaining in my case was a one last unexposed plate. Motioning Mr. Miles to follow me and whispering a hint in his ear, I extended the camera tripod again and walked over to set it a few feet in front of the august assembly.

"Your Honor, if you please!" I called out to them, indicating the camera with a flourish. "Ladies and gentlemen. Might I offer a congratulatory photograph to mark the occasion?"

The participants were easy to persuade, and as they jostled into a pose by seniority and lifted their cups to prepare for the moment, I threw the photographer's cloth over my head, peered through the lens, and was gratified to see an uninvited dignitary in sackcloth coat and hunting cap slip in at the far side, hoist a cup just long enough for the exposure, then drain it swiftly as the shutter closed. My mysterious companion was off just as swiftly toward the waiting omnibus.

"Thank you all," I said, packing up and making my way to the wagon as well—inconspicuously, I hoped.

Mr. Miles, along with his belongings and mine, was slouched in the first bench and nonchalantly packing tobacco into a distinctive pipe as I swung in beside him. "Driver," I said, "if you'd be so kind to take us back into the city to have these photographic plates developed posthaste, the Mayor will be most grateful, and here's a dollar to make it worth your trouble."

The driver, more than eager to comply, proved a most willing guide as well, for he soon delivered us past the teeming livestock yards and through the throngs to the corner nearest Usher's Photographic Supply and Service, which appeared to be situated conveniently amid an industrial section chock-a-block with saloons.

"My sincere appreciation for the errand," I said to the man, "and please remind His Honor that I shall—I shall call on him tomorrow afternoon at City Hall! Good day."

After making arrangements with the film laboratory and, in the bargain, leaving behind my camera apparatus with them for an adjustment after the jostling it had taken throughout my journeys, I devoted my attention to choosing a spot for my companion and me to quench our thirsts. The need was growing dire, and I feared his strength would not hold out despite his stoicism.

We would not have to look far, though crossing the street in the press of buggies and pedestrians appeared a near impossibility. I had not expected Fort Worth to be such a metropolis, I remarked to my companion, but receiving no answer, turned to find him leaning against the wall and pointing his pipe upward at a shingle hanging from a crude wooden awning.

"The Standard," said he. "Seems as good a sign as any."

We found the Standard to be no less crowded than the streets and plank sidewalks outside, and every bit as noisy. A flagging Mr. Miles with his rucksack rested his arm across my shoulder for support. I registered the leanness of the man's frame, despite his height; his thin limbs put me in mind of the sections of a surveyor's chain, as apt to fold up at any second and collapse.

I hefted my own bags, assisted him as best I could, and pushed through the clot of workingmen seeking refreshment.

The dim and smoky bar was packed with patrons, even on a Wednesday—stock drovers, mechanics, pipefitters, railroaders, to gauge by their garb. Everyone seemed to have laid out of work to celebrate. I peered through the fog in search of an unoccupied seat and, spying a table where one of the party had just set down his empty glass and made to leave, shoved toward it, supporting my lanky burden.

Suddenly a figure bumped into me and sent me reeling into the empty seat, where Mr. Miles slumped practically in my lap. I looked up at the fellow, who started to apologize but instead exclaimed, "Hooper? Frankie Hooper?"

The voice and visage took me back instantly to medical-college days, where before the war those features had belonged to a certain champion pugilist.

"Samuel Stamford!" I stammered, struggling to free myself from the awkward posture. "Well, if I had ever imagined someone I might encounter by chance in a Fort Worth bar—"

"It wouldn't likely be the man who fought for the other side, now, would it?!" said Stamford.

"I must say I'm glad to see you hale and hearty," I shouted up to my long-ago classmate, as I remained immobilized beneath my baggage and Mr. Miles's catatonic figure.

Stamford cleared his throat and angled in to get a better look at the wraithlike personage grasping my shoulder in his unconscious embrace, then backed off with a shrug. "Ah, well, Hooper," he said, "if that's the way it is, it sure explains a lot about, you know . . . why the Judge kicked you out. But hey, it's all right by me."

"It's not like that, Stamford, you idiot," I protested, nonetheless wondering how it was that rumor seemed to outrun even the speed of the train. "Listen, my friend here needs a seat and some refreshment."

Stamford's talents proved useful. He promptly lifted a drunk cowpoke from the chair next to me. The poor dude mumbled "W-was just leavin'" before swiftly disappearing.

I eased Mr. Miles into the still-warm seat. Stamford clamped a hand on the man's shoulder with a "How ya doin', chum?" The wince on Miles's blanching face did not escape me.

I half rose to get a waiter's attention. Stamford applied his skills once again, however, collaring the hapless server, forcing an about-face, and wresting the damp bar towel from his arm. He tossed it to me, and I applied it to Miles's brow.

"Hey, Bub. These gents need a drink," said Stamford, flashing a fiver from his pocket.

"Water, please," I said. "Two. With ice if you have it."

Miles, revived by the towel, piped up with surprising energy. "Jameson's. Neat. Double," he managed to eke out before going nearly slack again. His collar pulled up around his face, my strange companion hardly spoke as Stamford and I traded accounts of what had transpired in our lives since college, in the decade following the war that had interrupted both our studies.

At last our long-awaited glasses arrived. Miles, reenergized, downed his whisky in one smooth draught. I pressed him to drink the water too; though it had been a good twenty minutes now since we'd come in out of the sun, his brow still appeared flushed and hot.

Thinking to check him for fever, I leaned down to retrieve the thermometer from my satchel, when I felt the rush of a heavy object fly through the air where my head had just been and heard the sound of glass shattering against the wall behind me. The general cacophony hushed for a fraction of a second before the target of the bottle shouted an obscenity, leapt up with his chair in hand, and charged the assailant, who was headed our way.

All at once the barroom broke out in a chaos of shouts and smashing chairs and flying fists. Stamford took out one of the combatants with a quick uppercut, but other fights had ignited too, and I feared he would jump into the collective fray.

Mr. Miles sat to attention and reached under his coat, where I saw him withdraw a small derringer from a pocket. He had no chance to use it, though, as a gunshot from behind us took out the main chandelier light and a booming voice called for order.

"Keep it peaceable, boys," warned the shooter. He reached down to give me a hand up from where I crouched under the table. "You okay, sir?" he asked.

I nodded and thanked him, noting the silver star on his vest. I straightened my jacket and tie as the lawman refocused his attention to the downed man, who was regaining consciousness. But he turned back round in a double-take.

"Cap'n Miles? That you?"

As stunned as I had been at each of this day's unfolding revelations, this one was the strangest yet. *Captain?* Had I heard right?

"Billy McDonald," cried Miles, "what brings you out this way?" He stretched out his arm stiffly and proffered a handshake.

"Here to help keep the peace in the Panther City," said the man with the badge. "Whole town has gone barking mad."

"That would seem to be an accurate assessment." Miles lowered his voice to a whisper that only the two of us could hear, as Stamford was momentarily scoping about for another waiter. "You'll keep this between us?"

"Sure," said McDonald, "but I reckon the colonel would be glad to know you're back."

"I imagine so. But there might be a—better timing for that, shall we say." He winced in pain, rolling his shoulder.

I interjected, "Gentlemen, I haste to observe that Captain Miles here is likely in need of some rest. Might there be a hotel nearby?"

"Ha," said McDonald. "Not one I'd recommend here on the south side, even if you could find rooms available."

"Quite agreed," said Stamford, reentering the conversation. "Say, I know of a situation that might be worth a look if it's still available. A suite of rooms on Houston Street just vacated by a fellow I know. Splendid landlady, Mrs. Simpson is, and an excellent cook in the bargain."

Miles asked, "This Mrs. Simpson, would you say is she discreet?"

"A widow woman of impeccable character. She lives in the basement quarters. Has a son of ten or thereabouts who runs errands, keeps the coal stocked, and the like, after school."

"She has no aversion to the violin?"

"None as I know of. I'll bet the place won't last long on the market. I'd see you fellows uptown if you're interested?"

"A capital plan," said Miles, and Stamford volunteered to step out and flag down a hack.

McDonald took his leave, too, after asking Miles if he planned to be in the area for a while.

"I think you could safely count on it," Miles responded. "But just do me a favor and don't let on at Griffin for the time being."

"You'll know where to find me," said McDonald, hastening back to his duty.

Having the benefit of my companion's undivided attention once more, I prodded for more information. "Captain?"

"It's a long story," he replied. "One I'll be glad to share with you once we are in less public environs."

I left two singles on the table and we shoved our way back out in the sunshine to find Stamford holding a cab for our use. The three of us squeezed in with our assorted baggage and watched the mobs roil away behind us as the driver urged his pair uphill. Soon the hubbub gave way to a more purposeful din, of drays and draft horses and wagons engaged in the urgency of commerce. We flowed with the traffic for some nine or ten blocks, then turned off the wide thoroughfare onto another busy street, turned a corner, and stopped at a handsome two-story brick structure identified in large gothic letters as M. Lewis & Son, Bootmakers.

I cast a glance at Stamford, wondering if this were some interim errand. But he motioned us out of the cab, and said he would return soon, as he pointed across the board sidewalk and indicated a separate entrance at one edge of the building. Its heavy oaken door, flanked by sidelights, opened onto a narrow foyer and a set of stairs. Seventeen of them, I counted silently and wearily as I brought up the rear behind Miles, who was growing unsteady on his feet.

More alarming than that, I could not mistake the sign of a worse condition than I had imagined. For there on the dark-stained treads fell one . . . two . . . three drops of blood. Something, I knew, was quite wrong.

On the landing was a wooden bench where we gladly sat. I turned to inquire of my companion what must be the matter, but he only raised a hand to silence me, shut his eyes and declined his head to rest against the wall. I found myself in a quandary regarding my duty as a physician, but the man's demeanor brooked no overture toward any examination. At any rate Stamford quickly returned, bringing with him the aforementioned Mrs. Simpson, I presumed, and a link of keys.

The woman was solicitous and efficient as she unlocked the entry and showed us into a large sitting room whose compelling features were a well-proportioned hearth to my right, and to my left a spacious bay window affording an excellent view of the streetscape below. She seemed to dismiss the peculiar Miles, who made his own assessment in silence, hands clasped behind his back, and instead focused her narration toward me.

"I expect the arrangement of rooms is suitable for bachelor quarters," the landlady explained. "It is furnished with the basics, as you see. Plenty of space here for reading, dining—there's no kitchen, but my son and I are happy to prepare simple meals, and there are many saloons and eateries in the vicinity. There is one bedroom here, off the main room"—she pushed open a side door onto a ten-by-twenty chamber that also had windows facing south, and a generous-sized closet—"and above in the attic you'll find a second bedroom, a bath, and a large storage area that could function as an office or study if you were so inclined."

I wondered briefly at the wisdom of jumping into such an arrangement, but the prospect of perhaps opening a medical practice in this sunny, conveniently situated space in a popular quarter, with room above for a library, was beginning to sprout in my imagination.

I reasoned, too, that having come here on nothing more than flight and a whim in any case, I might easily have landed in even less propitious circumstances. As I opened my mouth to pose a short list of questions for Mrs. Simpson and ask to examine the quarters above, my companion spoke up.

"We'll take it, madam," said he, staring out the big bay window.

At the very least I had been ready to inquire about terms, and perhaps to negotiate some matter to our advantage, but I found myself again forestalled.

"Send up the lease, please, and Doctor Hooper here will see to it you receive a signed copy along with the first month's rent, plus an extra as guaranty."

Mrs. Simpson appeared pleased if puzzled at this, and replied, "Why, thank you, sirs, that I will. Welcome to 221B Houston Street." With that she handed over the keys and departed, followed by Samuel Stamford and his promises to pay us a visit soon.

I stood there bags in hand with a new address and many, many more questions.

"I apologize for the impositions," said my new roommate, his breath now coming in gasps. "I assure you . . . that my funds in the bank are sufficient, but I arrived with pockets devoid of cash. I shall fill you in on all details satisfactorily in due time, I hope." He removed his coat and hat, shook them straight, and hung them beside the door and began unbuttoning his shirt, which was soaked in sweat; and as he turned toward the wall I could see that it was also dotted with blood.

"Most urgently," he said, "I am in need of medical assistance. And you are a doctor." This he stated not as question but fact.

"I never did ask how you knew?" I said even as I pulled off my own coat and laid it across the nearest chair, rolled up my sleeves, and searched around for wash basin and pitcher. "I don't recall saying."

"Your bag stamped with your name and M.D. was sufficient evidence, even before you traded reminiscences with your colleague from university," Miles explained, as he proceeded to stretch out upon the long dining table and turn onto his stomach. "Now if you would be so kind as to go over and reach into my coat pocket," he directed, "you will find a small phial of liniment."

I dried my hands and complied. I found the glass tube; there was no label on it. I removed the stopper and detected an aroma of something familiar . . . a sharp, peppery scent that took me back to treks through South Texas chaparral pastures with my father. What came to me was . . . greasewood?

"Creosote ointment," Miles said, his voice growing hoarser. He implored me to apply it to a nickel-sized wound below his shoulder blade that was situated just out of his own reach. The ugly half-healed sore was suppurating, and alarming streaks of red radiated from the rotted skin around it. I retrieved a cotton swab from my kit, cleaned off the pus and dirt from the site as gently as I could manage, then took another, dipped it into the phial, and applied the dark substance to the area around the wound.

Miles winced and gripped the table edge, but said, "Directly on it, if you can. Quickly, before the landlady returns."

Ignoring my patient's discomfort I swabbed the preparation as deeply into the open wound as I dared without knowing more specifics, repeatedly until I emptied the container.

Miles sighed, rested but for a moment, then slipped back off the table and, sweating copiously, rearranged his soiled shirt. "I've been treating it as best I could for nearly a month, but I fear that part of a bullet remains, close to the bone."

"A bullet?! Then that explains a great deal," said I, having seen precisely what sorts of damage ammunition could wreak on human flesh. "You had no benefit of a surgeon?"

"I hope you yourself will be able to tend to that momentarily—presuming I survive that long. For now, there is one more thing."

I must admit to having become even more greatly alarmed at the prospect of performing an ad hoc operation, in a strange city and lacking hospital privileges, but this man was clearly in need of care, and I did as requested.

"In my carpetbag you'll find a small parfleche—yes, there, in the inside pocket. Bring it here, please."

Miles retrieved from the deerskin packet a grayish-green piece of dried cake, moistened it with his spittle, and worked it into a paste. I watched as he placed portions of it between his jaw and cheek, as one might do a hank of tobacco, and chew steadily until all of it had been consumed. He offered no insight as to its composition, but sat straight and trancelike in the hardback chair until we heard the anticipated knock at the door.

I met Mrs. Simpson on the landing, hoping to dispatch the business of the lease and bank check quickly. But the woman insisted on both tenants' signatures on the document, and I was obliged to permit her in the room to obtain that of Miles. She did not dally after catching a whiff of his liniment, and backed away as I declined her repeated offer to send up a tray of sandwiches for supper.

"There is only one thing I might ask before you go, madam," Miles interjected, eyes half closed.

"What is that?"

"You live in the basement apartment, is that so?"

"Why, yes."

"Do you perhaps treat the perimeter of your rooms with carbolic acid?"

"I do, sir, to keep away the rattlers and copperheads."

"Indeed. Could your boy be entrusted to bring me up a pint of it?"

"Well, for certain he's a careful one, but a poison that potent, I'd handle myself."

"Then set it right outside the door, would you? I must admit to a terrible fear of serpents." I could not tell whether he was playing the Hamlet, or truly meant this.

"I'll see to it right away," she said as she exited, surely wondering what maniacs had taken up residence in her building.

I shut and bolted the door and returned to tend my patient.

"Now the extraction must proceed," he said. "You'll want to heat a kettle. Bring a fresh bedsheet. Your instruments. A supply of bandages. A clean cravat, if you can spare it. And whisky."

"I am not certain you're in any condition for a drink, even a medicinal one," I responded.

"No, sir. The whisky's for you."

"Hmmph." I set aside indignity and skepticism, though, and started a charcoal fire in the grate. Soon the kettle was boiling, and I fetched the jar of carbolic as Miles instructed me.

He had laid the clean sheet across the table, and again undressed. He then began patting his hands lightly with a bandage dipped in the acid, and directed me to do the same. In a china dish he set the acid-soaked cloth, which he said would need to be pressed into his wound when the time came.

"I presume in scalpel and suture technique you need no prompting," he said wryly as he turned himself face down on the table once more. "Now, muzzle me with that necktie and get on with it."

Those were the last words I heard him speak before I undertook the operation. Steeling myself to ignore the man's pain, I cut deep through his thin skin and clamped off a blood vessel, then probed down to the scapula until I located the offending piece of metal and extracted it with forceps. Before attempting to sew the ragged mess back together, I applied the searing acid just as told, and hoped I had not violated my Hippocratic oath by doing so.

My patient passed out at last and the tension in his muscles went slack, making the suturing easier. I checked his pulse and breathing until I was satisfied he yet lived. I found blankets with which to cover the patient where he lay still as a cadaver.

I mopped up the blood before it could permanently stain Mrs. Simpson's oak floors, and I disposed of dead tissue and the bullet fragment in the jar with the remaining acid.

I exhaled deeply, left Mr. Derrick Miles to sleep on the dining table, dug out the bottle of Jameson's from his bag and took a long slug of it, and slumped onto the settee by the dwindling hearth, wondering again what in hell I had gotten myself into.

Chapter 2
THE ART OF DEDUCTION

{*In which Hooper learns something of Miles's pursuits.*}

I MUST HAVE SLEPT, and I must have done so longer than I thought possible in a sitting position, for when I awoke my lower extremities were numb, my mouth felt as though it were made of plaster of Paris, and my backside was still positioned in the same unfamiliar armchair in which I had planted it following a most unusual medical intervention.

It must have been day, or almost daybreak at least, for dim ladders of suffused light were exposed on the ceiling, having passed upward through the slats of the blinds. The presence of Venetian blinds at first confused and fooled me. I recalled an afternoon in a certain drawing-room, the perfume of magnolia blossoms floating in a Dresden bowl filled with water on a walnut side table, the turn of an ankle slightly visible beneath a crinoline petticoat—a style some years out of fashion, for the war's exigencies lingered long in the South, but that made the beauty of the moment all the more poignant.

I could not place the aroma, however. I had expected that possibly breakfast was being prepared in the always-busy kitchen across the breezeway of my mother's white-columned house on the bay, and had scorched. I flinched my nose and flexed my right arm, and as I came more fully awake realized instantly that the odor was not of food, but of something more pungently organic than pork sausage, and as I blinkingly forced open my eyes, panicked to find my newly rented quarters hazy with smoke.

Recalling with a shock that I was not alone in this foreign place, I leapt up and sought out my recently acquired roommate. Yesterday's events all rushed back to me . . . the train, the saloon, the strange companion from whose shoulder I had removed a bullet.

I peered through the fog.

The man was not on the table where I had left him. I hurried over to check the door. Still locked. I turned the key and threw open the door to clear some of the cloud, wondering if I should flee immediately.

A series of coughs suddenly emanated from behind a latticework screen near the far window. The fog in my head cleared and I dashed toward it, fearing my charge had collapsed, or worse.

I found Derrick Miles seated, legs crossed rather serenely underneath him, on a large ottoman cushion behind the screen, enveloped in smoke emanating from a vessel of some sort that he held in his hand. He was still naked from the waist up, wearing a towel around his head like an old swami, and facing the window, which I swiftly opened.

"Great Scott, man! We were about to be asphyxiated!"

"Quite the contrary, Doctor," Miles replied as I struggled to catch my breath. "I am well on the road to healing, thanks to your ministrations and a touch of native medicine whose salutary effects you should soon be feeling, yourself."

"Native medicine?" I barked at him. "Poppycock." I leaned out the extended window and took in lungfuls of outside air blessedly moist from overnight rain. A lamplighter on the sidewalk below looked up at me quizzically from his rounds of extinguishing lanterns, and I drew back in and shut the sash most of the way again.

Without altering his posture Miles lifted the vessel, a clay bowl of some sort, toward me. "Breathe in."

"What is it?" I croaked.

"Trust me." These words, I must admit, instilled alarm. Yet I had indeed already trusted this strange man with much, and I was not unsympathetic to his curious methods and apparent intellect.

I leaned toward the bowl and took a sniff, feeling a bit foolish as I did so, rather like a cat investigating a dead bird. I found the odor piquant, not unpleasant. Having set aside my fears of a house aflame, I did feel relieved enough, and I inhaled more deeply. In the moment, I noticed that the clay bowl featured a mouthpiece attached, in the form of a pipe, from which its owner then proceeded to take a long draught of the inhalant.

He closed his eyes in a meditative pose and remained so as the sun began to peek over the window ledge and the July dawn turned to day.

As for me, first tentatively and then fully, I breathed more deeply the gray air around me, and felt the chains that had bound me to disappointment and regret begin to loosen. For the first time in some weeks I looked forward to the coming hours with more expectancy than vague dread.

I pulled up a chair beside him and ventured a bold question. "Captain Miles, I think it's high time—if we are going to share lodgings without it regularly sparking anxiety in my brain to the extent that I must resort to homeopathy to settle it—you told me more about your aims and occupation. You know something of mine, having guessed it upon our first encounter."

"Guessed it!" he snorted, nothing moving except his lips and prominent Adam's apple. "I deduced it. From some obvious evidence, as I've said. Though there were other clues that told me more about your past, as well."

"Yes, obvious evidence, I agree. But what more could you possibly glean from such a brief encounter?"

"You hail from the coast and have been traveling twenty-one days. Though you had no certain destination in mind, you were not planning to return home for a long while."

I shot a glance his way. "What is your game, man? Who sent you to spy on me?"

He laughed, somehow without moving his head. "Spy, that's rich. Perhaps it's you who have taken part in tailing *me*. But no, I assure you, as illustrious a physician as you may have been back in Galveston, Texas, my own marks appear more often in the headlines."

"You are correct in those matters, then. How?"

Miles took another long draught on the pipe before responding. "Your light-colored cotton jacket, summer trousers, and straw boater yesterday indicated the wardrobe of a man arriving from southerly parts, as did the three-week-old copy of the *Galveston Daily News* protruding from your pocket. You had not arrived at Eagle Ford on your own horse, as your tan boots were perfectly clean and shined. Nor had you driven your own buggy there; thus you had hired the journey, and had the means and leisure to do so. You possessed a costly camera outfit, yet the doctor's bag argued against the likelihood of photography as a profession; thus, here was a serious hobbyist with autonomy over his schedule and an interest in the arts.

"Truly, you have hit the nail on the head," I said. "But I think I am simply being more transparent than I realized."

"Moreover," he continued, "you carried a large bag sufficient for more than an overnight stay. And since you took pains to bring that much along, it's likely you'd left nothing back in your hotel room—therefore were prepared not to return even though your options for traveling on westward or northward in comfort from where you stood were few—thus I detected a man who, though generally prepared and unflappable, could be enticed by what Walpole, I believe it was, once called 'serendipity.'"

I kept my silence, as I felt the probe enter more deeply into my own motives than I had admitted even to myself.

Miles gesticulated with his free hand as though he were exhibiting a chalkboard or offering a tour of some cabinet of wonders. "Let us examine more of this man's mind, and look to his past history, shall we? The high polish of his sensible boots in a dusty climate hints at a military discipline. As does the unfussy style but heedful trim of his hair and moustache. These and the already-noted medical training will be soon confirmed by a chance encounter with an old schoolmate. One observes that he favors his left leg slightly—an almost imperceptible limp—yet he uses no walking stick. His injury is a few years healed. Therefore the Civil War. The schoolmate says 'on the wrong side'—thus a Union loyalist, perhaps one of abolitionist bent. He has made a conscious choice to break with his Southern clan. When he briefly consults his pocket watch to check his photograph's exposure time, one observes on its gold-alloy case a masonic emblem worn almost smooth; a token bequeathed to him by his father, who has passed away. His uncalloused hands exhibit clipped and burnished nails; he removes a handkerchief folded just-so from his breast pocket, and uses it to polish the watch then dab the sweat from his brow before refolding and replacing it. The gentleman wears no wedding ring; so his proper grooming habits have been instilled in him by his mother, a Yankee, perhaps, of good breeding. But even more may be discerned of the state of his romantic life once he leaves his partly opened valise on the floor beside the table where he is unexpectedly preparing to do surgery on a needy patient. Shall I continue?"

I began to register the heat of the morning on my face. I stared straight ahead in self-consciousness bordering on mortification. How much closer could he come to hitting the mark?

"This merciful doctor carries a Schell leather bag that can be only a few years old but inside it is an army medic's field kit dating to the 1860s, which he clearly prizes for its sentimental value as he instead selects newer instruments from the bag. A winter cloak is tucked into the bag just so—yes, he does expect to be away for a long duration—and a carte de visite portrait of a fetching woman is laid atop it with care. Beside the picture and bookmarked some thirty pages in is a copy of Hardy's *Far from the Madding Crowd* plus a well-thumbed volume of Mrs. Browning's *Sonnets from the Portuguese*. As the man is not dressed in mourning, no other explanation is possible than that of a broken heart."

I let silence serve as affirmation.

"One last matter," said Miles. "When the bar fight broke out, you reached automatically toward your hip, a reflex action in someone who has seen military action. But you found no sidearm there. This, I said to myself, was a former junior officer neither looking to find himself in any danger, nor fleeing from the law; had his training and field experience been in the infantry or cavalry, he would not have been as likely to leave his gun behind. Thus a doctor or medic in the army corps who has retired from service and found his niche now in a rewarding private practice. Experienced, predictable, responsible, fiscally dependable. I had no difficulty in accepting you as a suitable co-lodger. The perfect flatmate, I must say, for a misanthrope."

I paced about and pondered his assessment for a moment, pushing from my mind the true reason the old revolver lay at the bottom of Galveston Bay. I strode back toward the window, keeping my back turned and my mix of emotions hidden. This madman some indeterminate number of years my junior had read me more closely than ever had my university prefects, or commanding officer, or priest, or sainted mother. I wheeled about and tried him on one more item, half in jest.

"And my age, if you had to compete in one of those carnival games?"

"I'd place you a shade over thirty-five," he said, rising without looking in my direction. "You still have some speed in your step when called for and no gray on your head . . . though your hairline has begun to recede a tad . . . and you remain, regrettably, at a stage highly susceptible, in the vulnerable type, to disappointment in affairs of the heart."

"You have erred on but a single account," said I, striving for a levity to mask how close to the bone this stranger's assessment had struck.

"I challenge you to name it!"

"Only in calculating my age, as I have passed but nine birthdays on earth counting this year."

"Ha! February 29, then. Eighteen hundred and forty."

"Quick, I admit. How—as for yourself, *how* does one of your own apparent youth win at such a game?"

"It is no game, I assure you. I have a kind of intuition that has proved useful in cases of much greater complexity than this one. Observation with me is second nature, and I am able to retain and draw on a bank of specialized knowledge which I apply to any problem."

As he leaned closer to the window Derrick Miles proceeded to quote from memory as though he were reading from an invisible printed page. "'From a drop of water,' a certain writer once said, 'a logician could infer the possibility of an Atlantic or a Niagara without having seen or heard of one or the other. So all life is a great chain, the nature of which is known whenever we are shown a single link of it. Like all other arts, the Science of Deduction and Analysis is one which can only be acquired by long and patient study; nor is life long enough to allow any mortal to attain the highest possible perfection in it. Before turning to those moral and mental aspects of the matter which present the greatest difficulties, let the inquirer begin by mastering more elementary problems.'"

"What kind of venerable bombast is that?" I said, feeling quite free with my words now, after continuing to breathe in his exotic tobacco for the past half hour. "Who peddles such twaddle?"

Miles ignored my interruption. "'Let him, on meeting a fellow-mortal, learn at a glance to distinguish the history of the man, and the trade or profession to which he belongs. Puerile as such an exercise may seem, it sharpens the faculties of observation, and teaches one where to look and what to look for. By a man's fingernails, by his coat sleeve, by his boot, by his trouser knees, by the callosities of his forefinger and thumb, by his expression, by his shirt cuffs—by each of these things a man's calling is plainly revealed. That all united should fail to enlighten the competent inquirer in any case is almost inconceivable.'"

"What sort of 'case'?"

"Why, the sort by which I hope to make my living," he said plainly. "These rules of deduction which have aroused your scorn are invaluable to me in practical work."

"I'm sorry," I said incredulously. "I'm still impressed by the parlor game, but I confess I see no practical work to which you're referring."

"Perhaps, Doctor, you have heard something of the recent science of forensic medicine? By which it is possible to recreate the cause of an accident, or a death, or a crime, through minute and systematic observation of its circumstance? In the field of police work, and in the confidential service of governments, I have begun to find such a niche. You might call me a consulting detective. I've invented the job—I know of no other. And I myself am the author of the text I just quoted, which is forthcoming in *The Annals of Analysis.*"

He continued to gaze out the window but moved silently closer to it, remaining out of sight beside the draperies and tilting the blind downward for a better view. "You and I should probably set aside this, ahem, parlor game for now, and prepare for a visitor."

"Visitor? Who knows either of us is here?"

"Who indeed, man. Think of the circumstances that landed us here. What are the possibilities?"

"Well, there is the landlady Mrs. Simpson, who has probably retreated into hiding ... and her young son . . . and Sam Stamford . . ."

Miles turned and reached into his bag and withdrew out a cotton chemise, which he pulled over his head and tucked into the waist of his trousers with surprising fluidity. He strode to the hook where he had left his waistcoat, ran his fingers through his hair, and said, "In the time it takes one to mount seventeen stairs we should anticipate a knock from Ranger Billy McDonald. And where there are Rangers, there also are crimes."

I rolled down my sleeves and pulled on my own summer coat as I hastened to fling open all five of the room's tall windows.

"Doctor Hooper," said Miles, "I wager I'm about to consider my first case as a consulting detective in Fort Worth, Texas. You are welcome to sit in."

Chapter 3
MYSTERY IN THE THIRD WARD

*{In which one man dies under suspicious circumstances
and another disappears.}*

"HOW IN HEAVEN DO YOU FIGURE THIS?" I asked Miles as I took the measure of my face in the washstand mirror in the corner and toweled my hands dry. I smoothed my wrinkled collar as best I could.

"Simple observation," he replied. "All the while you and I were debating the virtues of reason, I followed the activity on the street below reflected in the curved window opposite us, through the blind. I could have described the fascinating movements from the lamplighter mounting his ladder at the corner of Houston and Third, to the milk wagon rounding the curb, bound for the bakery, to the newsboy departing from the *Democrat* office with his bundle of extras, to the woman arriving alone for an appointment at the law office, to the nineteen carts and fifty-seven horses that have passed since daybreak. Among this traffic McDonald stands out as the only person familiar to me."

"Incredible," I replied in amazement.

"Commonplace," said he, though I caught in his tone a hint of what might be pleasure at my admiration.

I had only another second to marvel at this extraordinary litany before a purposeful sound of boots approached the door, followed by a rapid knock.

Miles walked to the door a little stiffly and answered. "Billy McDonald, for the second time in less than twenty-four hours. To what do I owe the pleasure?"

"I'll get right to it, Derrick," he said, tipping his hat in my direction and handing Miles a folded paper from his vest pocket. "Our new city marshal is asking for you. It's on my recommendation, you understand, since I had the excellent good fortune of crossing paths with you. Seems he's found a bit of a puzzle with a dead body down in Hell's Half Acre this morning."

"Is that an unusual occurrence?" I interjected, recalling yesterday's escapade.

"Not really, Mister—pardon, I've forgotten your name?"

"Hooper. Doctor Frank Hooper."

"Right, yes. Well, Derrick, what you think? Want to give it a look?"

Miles looked up from the note and thrust it toward me, and I read aloud. "To Captain Derrick Miles—Sergeant McDonald tells me you're smart with tough cases. We have a delicate one at Rusk and 16th, discretion required. Deceased male, middle age, blood at scene, murder suspected for reasons I will discuss in person, but no wound, no robbery. If you would lend an opinion, I would be grateful and could make it worth your while. Yours truly, T. I. COURTRIGHT, MARSHAL."

"Discretion required, hm," said Miles. "Doubtless the street address figures in."

McDonald cleared his throat. "Around the corner from Mrs. Love's establishment. One of the cribs she provides for the girls, though she's already said no one was staying there last night—she had a work crew in to do some repairs and all the beds and furniture had been moved out a while back."

"Hard to do business without the essential tool of the trade, I suppose. Well, my friend, you're well aware how I feel about coming to the aid of local lawmen. They will have chased the least obvious theory regarding a crime to its most ludicrous conclusion, then cuff the least likely suspect, bruit it all about in the papers and try it in the court of public opinion—until someone with keener powers of deduction presents them with a superior—and correct—case and then waste the least time taking all the credit."

"Surely you don't hold the Rangers in such low esteem," said McDonald.

"Rangers? You're one of the few exceptions to the rule, Billy. But no, the problem with a Ranger is of a different sort. One never knows what color coat he might be wearing on a given day. He's as likely to shove his pistol between the ribs of your back as he is to draw it in your defense, depending on whose purse is paying. I'd think twice about setting off on that career path if I were you. But I digress. Who's this Courtright, pray tell?"

"New guy in town, recently arrived from East Texas. Wears his hair long, like the scouts. Says he's going to bring real law and order to this place."

"Admittedly I've been away for a few months, but during the past forty-eight hours I have not witnessed improvement."

McDonald, who seemed an earnest and upright sort of fellow, explained that Courtright had summoned a select few Texas Rangers, including himself, to aid in the program, which would likely take some time and coordination—and in voting corrupt politicians out of office.

"Buying or removing, you mean," Miles responded.

"Well, you 'n' I could debate that till Christmas," said McDonald. "Meanwhile we've got a dead councilman and somebody's blood spattered on a prostitute's floor, and daylight's burnin'. You in or you out?"

"Blood on the floor, you say." Miles sent a raised eyebrow in my direction. "If the good doctor will accompany us and put his medical training to use"— he cast a beckoning glance my way—"In."

Once again I found myself in the unwinnable situation of being unable to refuse.

The three of us shared a hack for the transit of approximately a mile down Houston Street to a fancy house—at least what I took to be such an establishment, as the two-story wooden structure stood out from a dozen others in a ramshackle block of shotgun cottages. Occupying a prominent street corner and painted bright violet, it sported a scrollwork shingle that read "Dollie Love's." We alighted from the cab into the humid haze and glaring sun. No one was about; this was not a morning part of town.

Madam Love's was not our destination, however. McDonald pointed around the corner and down the block. I followed as he marched on, but Miles lagged behind. I glanced over my shoulder to see what was keeping him. Hands clasped behind his back, he peered down at the still-damp earth as he paced forward, then back again, eyes ever downward. I thought at least one of us should make certain where we were going, and left him to his deliberations, which appeared to me more like those of an ambivalent suitor than a crack forensic examiner.

McDonald took no notice as I struggled to match his long, purposeful stride. He spoke as though to the air. "More hooligans in this cowtown than

Fort Griffin, and that's sayin' something," he mumbled. "Took us all night to round up the rowdies and clear the sidewalks, but the rain shower finally did the job for us. I was just settling down to enjoy a little shuteye. And then this."

"You won't mind my asking, mister, but as I was wondering earlier, is murder—so rare on the frontier? The tales I've heard . . ."

"This one is. Wait and see. And it's also a matter of who, if y'know what I mean. We're going the long way around to avoid undue attention. And here's the man we're meeting," he said, indicating a figure stepping out from the shadows of the porch we were approaching. "Now, where the heck is Derrick Miles?"

The subject of his query had caught up to us, and he was fuming. "The good fortune of a little rain at precisely the right hour of evening, and your crew of cakes and crushers have made such a hash of the site we'll scarcely be able to glean a thing from it," Miles mumbled. "Who did you say was in charge?"

"Timothy Courtright, known to most as Jim," replied a blond-bearded man with long, silky locks flowing from under a fawn-colored Stetson. "But you can call me Marshal." His thumbs hung in the loops of his belt, which supported a pair of holstered Colts, butts out, and though the morning was already turning steamy he hardly exhibited a sweat in his buckskin jacket. "I'll ask you to keep your opinions to yourself until you've seen the evidence."

Our companion retorted, "By the evidence I've already seen I believe you've ignored half of it. The scene couldn't have been damaged worse if a cattle drive had plowed right through it," came the rejoinder. "Derrick Miles. But you can call me Captain."

"Very well, Captain Miles. On the recommendation of your friend McDonald here I'll give you a chance. We're here to bring law and order to this town, and I aim to make good on my word. Your job—and I hope I'm a hundred percent clear on this—is to help me keep it."

With that the marshal led us up the wooden steps of the crib. "I have been on reconnaissance around the neighborhood, while McDonald went to fetch you. My man Garrigan is still on watch inside."

"And you each came here on horseback?" Miles asked.

"Yes, McDonald and I rode right down from the station after Deputy Garrigan, who was on duty in the ward, came in with the report soon after daylight."

"So you have had—hm, three hours to allow the scene to deteriorate before enlisting my help."

Courtright cleared his throat indignantly. "It's not, shall we say, an early rising neighborhood." He seemed to ponder the implications of that, then turned on his heel and headed up the steps to the porch. "I think we have done all that can be done. Let's get your take, shall we?"

"Yes, let's have a look at the room then." Miles strode into action, passing Courtright on the way up and leaving him with an astonished expression on his face. I hastened to follow.

The house was not one made for entertaining, judging by the short, bare-planked hallway, small parlor and half a dozen rooms—all standing empty—that put me in mind of a school dormitory, except for their lack of furnishings and, in each case, their rolled-up carpets and dirty floors. Each room featured a single sash of window, with panes blotted by the residue of coal smoke. But as we came to the end of the hall and passed the kitchen, a swinging door gave onto a spacious dining room.

By now, considering the steep slope of the hill away from the lane toward the river, we were at a second-storey level. Large trees shielded the view out its three windows and kept it in shadow, and the garish pattern of a mauve-and-brown wallpaper throughout lent it a gloom even at midmorning. Here and there strips of the paper had been pulled down, reminding me of torn ligaments, and beneath, the bone-colored plaster indicated water damage from the sagging ceiling. Drapes still hung on some of the windows. A thick film of wood and plaster dust lay over every surface.

"As I understand it, part of the roof had blown away in a storm. Renovations began on the place some months ago but came to halt when every workman in the city went over to the railroad project," Courtright said, following behind us.

As my eyes adjusted to the dim light, however, I made out two human figures already present. One, a short, cocky fellow wearing a ten-gallon hat and a badge, I took to be the deputy marshal. The other lay twisted and rigid on the floor, frozen in contortions as though he had been wrestling with a wild animal, eyes open, unblinking and fixed upon a plain wooden mantel on the side wall. On the mantel stood a red candle, cold in its pool of dried wax.

Miles walked around and bent toward the grim figure. I estimated the dead man to be in his late forties; to the extent I could make out his physical features in his posture of struggle, he appeared to be of medium height and portly body, with dark hair and trimmed beard. His hands, clenched in fear or pain, likewise conveyed good care and grooming. He wore a summer-weight black frock coat and embroidered waistcoat over a collared shirt, with striped trousers and black leather boots, all smeared with the whitish dust in which he had apparently rolled. A top hat lay on the floor beside him. The man looked familiar to me, though why this should possibly be so, I could not fathom.

His face, however, gave away an even more grievous look of agony, or horror, or both. Below the wide-staring eyes the nostrils flared, the lower jaw jutted outward, the tongue was extended through clenched teeth. It was a countenance unlike any I had previously witnessed upon the dead on battle-field or in operating theater.

The other man—the living one—stepped forward and handled Miles a social card. "Daimmler's the name."

"You say there is no wound, Deputy Daimmler?"

"No, not me, I'm Garrigan. This unfortunate fellow here. One Ernst Daimmler, councilman of the City of Fort Worth. He had this in his breast pocket."

Miles examined the calling card and handed it back. Now I knew why the figure seemed familiar—I had glimpsed him only yesterday among the dignitaries on the ceremonial platform at the railroad celebration! As had Miles, even more closely than I.

I studied the dead man's countenance closely. His face reflected a horror only lately seen, or experienced, I knew not which, because for the life of me I could not spot any sign of violence upon the body which would explain the fear, or loathing, or disgust, or pain, expressed in its features and fixed gestures. Among the emotions captured there might have also been a terrible hatred, which I detected from the set of the mouth, hard and clenched, a look echoed in the arrangement of the right hand as well.

Miles leaned down and pulled the body over onto its back, and I could see that the left hand, stretched out at the end of a muscular arm, mir-rored the rigid, twisted branch of the right. I was put in mind of the tough, thorny limbs of the mesquite tree; not the plant's thin and fast-growing outer branches but the broad outgrowths of the ironlike trunk, which hide gray spikes at every turn. This same sharpness, and danger, of that living form I felt from Daimmler's cold and crumpled body.

"This'll stir up the press, to be sure," said Deputy Garrigan. "Daimmler's a bigwig in politics. He's got friends in high places but he's also got enemies by the score. A dozen men might easily find 'emselves on the list of suspects."

"Perhaps you'll draw up that list for me," said Miles as he turned the body back on its original side.

"You bet."

"And you're certain there's no wound anywhere on the body?"

Courtright jumped in. "Not that I could see, and the clothing isn't torn anywhere. But we'll look more closely when we get him to the morgue. The meat wagon should have arrived by now."

"Where is your morgue, by the way?"

"Next to the station on Main, in the back room of the hospital. We'll get this stiff loaded up as soon as you're satisfied here."

"And no other sign you'd take for a clue?" Miles asked Courtright. "Especially in light of—all this?" Miles gestured to the liberal pools and sprays of red that were hardly dry on the bare floorboards, but pasty like uncured pigment on an artist's palette.

"Positive," replied Courtright and Garrigan at once.

"That answers that, then," said Miles. "The blood belongs to another. A murderer perhaps; a killer for certain."

I watched Miles's next actions with interest, curiosity, considerable concern even, for I feared that in his extreme movements he would dislodge his fresh stitches. He knelt and palpated, measured against the breadth of his hand, smelled, felt folds of clothing, lifted and laid back portions of a sleeve or coattail. Only I, among those in the room, apparently detected any slight halting as he bent, turned, or stood.

Finally, he sniffed the dead man's lips, then moved steadily to the victim's feet, where he paid an almost inconsequential glance at the dust-covered soles of the boots. He stood with relatively little effort and brushed plaster particles from his own hands. Either he was masking pain or, as I'd begun to expect, felt it little during the thrill of a chase.

"I suppose you have checked the pockets?"

"Everything we found is right here," said Garrigan, handing over a small satchel. He called out each item from a list as Miles withdrew them one by one, looked them over, and put them back. "Gold pocket watch, case no. 12149, by Potter of Geneva. Gold Albert chain with Bavarian crest on fob.

Gold stick pin with onyx hound's head. Two-cigar case, black leather, empty. Calling cards engraved with Ernst F. Daimmler, Fort Worth, a name which corresponds with the monogram on the shirt cuffs. A blank, unsigned bank draft and four ten-dollar notes in a metal money clip, same initials. And this telegram."

Miles took the paper slip from him and read it aloud. " 'ENGINE IN F.W.—S.' What do you make of it?"

"I'll tell you exactly what," said Courtright. "It means the crime had something to do with the arrival of that damned train here in our fair city yesterday. Every member of the city council was there to meet it, and I've already made up a list to interrogate. I have also sent word to the stationmasters back down the line and put out inquiries about a Mr. S."

"What sort of details did you request?"

"Just information in general—we cast a wide net on this one."

"Nothing more particular? Was there nothing else that seemed to bear on the situation?"

Courtright shrugged. "I asked Daimmler's secretary if he had traveled recently, what was recorded in his appointment book, how his health had been, that sort of thing. Routine."

"Nothing else? Is there no circumstance on which this whole case appears to hinge? His associates and interests, perhaps?

"I have said all I have to say," said Courtright, in an offended voice.

Miles offered the almost imperceptible noncommittal shrug and down-turned corners of the mouth that I was coming to recognize as his regard of utmost disdain, a gesture that must have been often lost on others. "The body has not been moved at all, correct?"

"Just rolled over and back, like we did a few minutes ago, but not removed," Courtright assured him.

"Then my work is done here, and you may transport the departed Mr. Daimmler to your cold storage."

Courtright gestured to Garrigan, who whistled to the other deputy, Crow, who had been keeping watch outside the front door. Crow shuffled in, carrying a long, wooden-handled stretcher that I recognized as an Army-issue Halstead. He and Garrigan unfolded the muslin litter on the floor, spreading it like a scroll, then, grunting, together lifted the dead weight onto it and hoisted the contraption by its poles at both ends. The victim's body tilted as

Crow almost lost his grip. Garrigan compensated with a jolt, and as he did a shiny circle of metal spilled from an unseen fold of the victim's vestments and hit the floor with a tinny plink.

"What's 'is?" cried Garrigan, almost losing his own corner of the stretcher. The men set the body down once more, and Courtright reached down for the object.

"Here's a clue for sure," the marshal said as he turned it between his fingers in the diffused light. I stepped over to the window and pulled back the dust-covered velvet drapes for a better glimpse.

McDonald reached for the artifact and read the engraving borne on it. "ONE HOUR WITH RACHEL."

"Well, this guy was a prospective client, I'd say," offered Garrigan. "But what's the big deal to get murdered over?"

"Looks like he might've been interrupted before redeeming the chit," added Courtright wryly, "or maybe he's in on running the racket—or the woman was the killer. This certainly complicates matters, doesn't it?"

"You're sure it doesn't simplify them?" observed Miles.

Courtright took the items and the evidence pouch and called out to his deputies before turning to go, "You lads get the body out of here, *pronto*, as the vaqueros say. Let's avoid prying eyes."

I took one last survey around the room where violent death had so recently taken place. No matter how many times I had faced it, and whether the mass mortality of the battle front, or amid family gathered at a bedside, or the solitary last struggle of the sick or injured, I could not witness the extinguishment of the last flicker of human life without some latent prayer long ingrained springing to my silent lips, a thanks for the end of suffering and a sincere wish for the deceased's peace in their hereafter, whatever their known god or impenetrable universe might hold in store.

Miles broke my reverie with his own assessment. "They would amuse me, these local lawmen, if it weren't such a damned serious business. There is more to this case than meets our eyes, Hooper, but the crime and the motive are clear as day and the perpetrator is certainly still free to do more harm."

"You do suspect murder, then?"

"Suspect? I know with certainty!" he said, chuckling to himself. As we were turning to leave, I gathered he might have been on the verge of reveal-ing all to our unenlightened brains when, with a rapid click of boot heels down the hall, Courtright appeared before us again.

He started to wave us away, but suddenly, staring above our heads, he motioned upward to the upper wall that had been in shadow upon our arrival an hour earlier.

"God damn! Have you seen *that?*"

Miles and I swiftly followed Courtright's gaze to a space above and to the right of the fireplace mantel.

"What do you make of it?" I asked. For there, executed in red-daubed letters eight inches tall, was a strange phrase.

R A C H E

"Well, it's obvious, isn't it? A message of jealousy, I'll warrant," exclaimed Courtright in triumph. "Whoever dispatched poor Daimmler must have been a rival for the attentions of our soiled dove Miss Rachel. Furthermore, it appears to have been written in his own blood, which as you've seen he lost a quantity of. Must have lost strength, too, before he had a chance to finish spelling out the name."

Garrigan had returned, mopping the sweat from his brow with a bandana, and had been listening to this exchange. "But why did the guy go to the trouble to write it way up there?"

Courtright offered his theory. "Well, you see that stub of a candle on the mantel? If it was lit last night, this might've been the brightest spot instead of the darkest."

"Why bother to do such a crazy thing at all, 's what I'm wondering," added McDonald.

"Find the woman, then find out who fancied her, and we'll have our man!" said the excitable Courtright.

Miles, meanwhile, had recommenced his pacing and surveying. At his full height he still had to stand on tiptoe to view the bizarre inscription through his magnifying glass. I held my breath as if willing my stitches in his shoulder to hold. He then bent and squatted, using the breadth of his hand as a gauge, and then stood again, pacing off trajectories in the much-disturbed dust. He appeared to be making mental notes and measurements but never committed a word to paper.

"You might think your methods offer something superior to the investigation, Captain," Courtright challenged him. "But I believe we can clear this up without your help after all. I'll be making a few inquiries shortly and fully expect to have the matter tied up before the afternoon paper goes to press!"

"Oh, that's a gas," replied Miles with a shake of his head and a barely concealed chuckle. "You indeed deserve full credit for everything you've been able to uncover on this case, sir. And I don't doubt you are correct that someone besides the dead man has left this hasty message—ruling out suicide, at least."

"But?" asked Courtright.

"They say that genius is an infinite capacity for taking pains," Miles remarked with a smile. "It's a very bad definition, but it does apply to detective work."

While McDonald appeared a bit sheepish at this proclamation, which must have done nothing to raise his own stock with the marshal in view of the trust he'd been extended, Courtright made no gesture to hide his derision. "I've taken up enough of your time, I think," he said to Miles, removing his hat and bowing deeply as he swept it almost to the floor and returned it to perch atop his flowing curls. "I'll be off now . . . . unless there's something else you're not sayin'?"

"Oh, there is plenty I'm not saying, gentlemen. But I wouldn't dream of interfering, or of imposing my admittedly uncommon approach upon the progress you are making on your own. If you should need my assistance at any point in the future, you now know where to find me, and when you do, you will find me willing and glad to help."

I had to turn away to the window to avoid betraying my amusement at my new friend's unappreciated sarcasm. I was beginning to understand something of this man's thoughts and actions myself—the thorough and careful habits of observation, and the precise application of logic to those observations. And that scared me.

Miles had one last request of the marshal. "I wouldn't mind asking a few questions of Deputy Garrigan when you leave, if you can spare him for a few minutes?"

"No skin off my hide," said Courtright. "His shift's done for the time being anyway. Deputy, when you're finished, try to find an hour for a siesta—in case we soon have an arrest to make!"

Miles nodded. "Very well then. As you prepare to make such an appre-hension, Marshal, you might well want the assistance of McDonald *and* your deputy, as your murderer is a trained assassin over six feet tall, strong and in the prime of life, with large feet and hands—oh, and reddish skin. He came here from the west and met his victim—whom he probably knew well—arriv-ing in a hack with four wheels that was drawn by a horse with three old shoes and one new one, on its off foreleg. You'll be looking for a man with a swollen nose, long fingernails, and longish, straight dark hair. Maybe those minor tidbits will help in your search."

Marshal Courtright glanced over at McDonald. "Where'd you say you found this nutcase?" he guffawed before shaking his head and turning down the hallway, bootheels clicking brusquely. He paused for a moment to call back, his words echoing through the empty rooms. "You're so sure murder's been done. What was the weapon, then?"

"Mm. Poison," Miles replied flatly, heading toward the exit and motion-ing us to follow. "And while there is most assuredly a Rachel involved," he said as he passed Courtright in the corridor, "I wouldn't look for her in the whorehouse, for she's been long in her grave. Vengeance, on the other hand, I suspect played a role. You're unfamiliar with the German, perhaps?"

"German?" said the marshal.

"*Räche,*" my companion and patient pronounced gutturally before leading us out into the midday light of a quarter starting to come alive. "Revenge. The motive was literally spelled out for you."

Chapter 4
THE MAN IN THE MOCCASINS

{In which Derrick Miles exhibits his methods of detection.}

GARRIGAN, SMIRKING, PULLED HIS HAT DOWN to shade his brow and followed Derrick Miles out into the bright sunlight. McDonald and I brought up the rear, leaving a dumbfounded Courtright to close up and secure the scene. It was his watch, after all. I tipped my hat good-bye to the marshal.

"Gentlemen," Miles said, "as it is almost noon I propose a bite of lunch and some liquid refreshment, if either of you knows a good eatery to recommend."

"If it's fancy hotel fare you're wantin', Miles, I wouldn't count on it around here," said McDonald. "But we could try Pritchard's Saloon, two blocks up and off the main street. The barkeep is known for his discretion. Besides, after yesterday's shenanigans we won't likely be welcomed back at the Standard anytime soon."

"Excellent judgment, Billy. Lead on."

The three of us followed him to the place, baking in the Texas sun as we moved along in anticipation of quenching our considerable thirsts. Miles, I noted, was walking stiffly, and I recalled that he had been standing for the better part of an hour as we had examined the murder scene. A soft leather seat would come none too soon for him. Or for myself.

We found Pritchard's place ideal, just as Billy McDonald had indicated. In one corner away from the window, opposite the poker tables that sat idle at midday, we found a generously upholstered half-moon bench surrounding a circular wooden table. Miles indicated the deputy should slide in first. He and McDonald took the seats on one end, while I took the end opposite. Deputy Garrigan would now be subject to our schedule, not his own, and I was beginning to understand that Miles, like a spider drawing its prey into the web, would not rest until he had pried out every scrap of useful information from his subject.

Miles signaled for a round of local brew, which the bartender promptly delivered. Garrigan quaffed while Miles sipped; McDonald said he'd appreciate a sarsaparilla instead. On the outside of this trio I was in prime position to watch and make careful mental notes.

Miles delved in. "Deputy, I am certain you'll be in for a commendation for your quick action in uncovering a murder of this ilk. Now, I keep wondering, how common do you think such a killing is in this cowtown, anyway?"

"Oh, I'd say, your ordinary shooting or cowboy brawl, about one or two a day, nothing unusual. Lovers' quarrel, rustler hanged, robber caught in the act, maybe once a week; accidental discharge of weapon resulting in death, every so often; your assassination, political or economic, somewhat rarer." The deputy paused for a moment, cogitating, and then added, "I've never seen a case quite like this, though—no assailant, no clear motive, no wound, no weapon."

Miles gave this assessment a moment's consideration. "Well, then we shall endeavor to reconstruct more of the circumstances that will identify all four elements. Would you start at the beginning of your first inclination that something was amiss, Deputy Garrigan, and give us your full recollection, omitting nothing while we all tuck into our bratwurst and beans?"

It was, to my astonishment, that very dish that appeared before each of us, as though Miles had conjured it by means of a spell.

"Very well, I'll do my best," said the man, who had already taken a first hearty bite of sausage. He finished chewing, laid his fork down, and began his account. "My shift runs from ten at night to six in the morning. I customarily tie up my horse at the livery on Tenth Street and go abroad on foot. By midnight last night, the rowdies in that area had quieted down from all their jollity, due to the Texas & Pacific and all, you know, and had settled up their bets and found either a house to spend their winnings on, or a doorway to sleep in. At one o'clock it began to rain a little, and I hoofed it back to the livery to get my oilcloth out of my saddle pack. I stopped at the corner of 14th and Rusk to talk with Billy McDonald here"—McDonald nodded assent—"and I remember that we both remarked we were surprised we hadn't needed to clap anyone in the calaboose so far. Maybe it had to do with the fact that all the hullabaloo had started earlier and the riffraff had worn 'emselves out on the earlier watch."

McDonald chuckled. "I couldn't agree more. You missed the action at the Standard Bar yesterday. What a circus!"

Garrigan continued his account, between bites of lunch. "Around four in the morning I had my coffee and made my rounds down to Hell's Half Acre. I passed Miss Polly's, where lights were still on in a few windows, but no hijinks seemed afoot. The cribs where the girls live—sometimes those can be trouble spots, but not a soul did I meet as I continued south and east toward the river.

"As I passed number 11, though, I believed I caught a flicker of light from a side window and I thought I'd better check for a squatter, or even a fire. When I got to the front stoop—"

"That's where you stopped and turned around and made haste across the street," said Miles. "Can you tell us why?"

Garrigan gave such a start mid-bite, he nearly choked. "Were you spying on me? How did you know that?!"

Here I interjected that I was certain, myself, that Miles had certainly not been abroad at that hour. "I assure you, Mr. Miles was resting comfortably upstairs at Houston Street, having endured a long day of ceremony related to the Texas & Pacific that you mentioned, and having that very afternoon secured a new address in the city. I—"

With a sideways look Miles stopped me before I could say more. Keeping his wounded shoulder against the soft bench back, he replied evenly, "Your bootprints, man. The mud preserved them just as clearly as it did the wheel tracks of the cab that had arrived four hours ahead of you.

"Well then. I—I'm not usually the sort given to visions of apparitions or fear of the departed," said he, "but in that moment a powerful sense came to me of a woman—a young woman—suffering a horrible sort of death, and it struck me just as I was about to lay my hand on the doorknob of that place, that it might have been the crib what was shut down for the case of typhoid this spring. Not that I believe in warnings from beyond the grave, mind you; but as I retreated I did wonder if my memory had saved me just in time from a careless mistake. I looked around for McDonald down the street, but I couldn't spy him through the drizzling rain and fog. No one else was about."

"So you did what, then?"

"Ha! You're so all-seeing, you tell me!"

"It's not my place to describe how you overcame your irrational presentiment; recalled that the house in question was not, in fact, the one shut down by health authorities but by recent storm damage requiring repair; and retraced your path to the door. This, my friend, is *your* testimony."

Garrigan cleared his throat and sat up straighter. "Remembering that nobody had a legal claim to being on the property at the time, I laid my hand on the knob and entered quietly. I drew my piece and proceeded down the hallway, looking into each room as I went. When I reached the parlor at the back I found its door partly open. I pushed on it with my foot, keeping my finger on the trigger. But it turned out I didn't need to be so cautious, because there wasn't a living soul in the room, just a candle—a red wax candle—flickering on the mantelpiece. By its light I saw—"

"Yes," Miles interrupted, "I already know every detail of what you saw. The dead body, which you walked around, and knelt down beside, before you went over and tried the kitchen door."

The deputy banged his fist on the table. "Enough of this game, man! Just tell me where you were hiding, to witness all this! Or maybe I should be clapping the cuffs on *you!*"

"Settle down, Deputy—I am one of the hounds and not the wolf, as Ranger McDonald here can attest. I am simply following the evidence left by your own bootprints on a dusty floor. Any one of you could do the same by the rigorous application of observation and a disciplined memory, crossed with the assiduous practice of deductive reasoning. Do you understand what I am saying?"

"Not sure I do, frankly."

"Then let me enlighten you all before we continue. If I laid out a particular circumstance—let us say, your restaurant meal is growing cold before you though you have eaten most of it, and your glass is almost empty—most men would be able to predict the next thing that will happen."

The waiter approached at that moment and asked, brusquely, "You gents done? Get you anything else?"

Before any of us could answer for ourselves, Miles replied, "Mr. Garrigan isn't terribly fond of the beans, and you can remove his plate, but I believe he would covet a second round of your ale. Now, anyone else, before this good man returns with our bill?"

We all shook our heads and slid our plates toward the server, who scribbled on his pad and reached to clear the dinnerware.

Miles resumed his lecture. "It is natural to infer, and even correctly predict, each step in a set of consequences and never think our brains have done anything extraordinary in their swift operation. Our actions often follow just as speedily. It is how Hooper here is already reaching to catch the empty glass that the waiter has unwittingly nearly knocked to the floor—"

He was quite accurate in that statement, as I was in the very course of action to prevent the vessel's crash. I handed the glass to the waiter with a helpful smile.

"Such prediction is what we often call instinct," Miles continued. "We expect Ranger McDonald here, in any instant that he might perceive a threat to law and order, to draw his pistol with accurate aim and compel his finger to fly to the trigger."

So suddenly did the interruption to our peaceful assembly occur, I took it in as a scene in a stage play, in which I was a member of the audience and not a participant.

"Pritchard, you spineless bastard," roared a voice from the open saloon door, "I've come to collect what you owe me." A second intruder was raising a long gun toward the mirrored bar back and the startled proprietor, but Ranger McDonald had already stood and drawn a bead on him with his Colt.

"Put your weapons down, boys," shouted McDonald, who appeared to me younger than the pair he was addressing. "This is a peaceful, public establishment. What's your beef?"

The man with the rifle, who showed no inclination to lower it, replied, "That man behind the bar cheated us on our bill yesterday. We just now done figgered it out."

"Then I'm sure we can settle this without injury," said McDonald.

"Yeah, and who are you to say so? This bidness is between us."

"Among us," I said without thinking. "There appear to be more than two involved." For my grammatical impetuosity I now found the gun aimed at my own head.

McDonald, already standing at the edge of our booth, crossed the floor in three long strides, his aim never wavering from a straight line to the gunman's temple. "Texas Ranger. Put the gun down. On the floor. Unless you care to spend the night in lockup."

By that time Deputy Garrigan, next to me, had also drawn his pistol and trained it on the other man.

"We just want our five bucks, and we'll go."

"This true, Mr. Pritchard? You have any change these fellows had a right to expect?"

The proprietor remained behind the relative safety of the bar as he replied, "Not in the least. I run an honest house here. Now, be off with you, before I have the law escort you to jail."

"Not so fast, Mr. Pritchard," said Derrick Miles, still seated. "If you wouldn't mind, I'd like to examine the bill for our own party before we depart to attend to our pressing business."

"Why, why—certainly." Mr. Pritchard signaled to the waiter to hand over the leather folder containing our tab. The boy made a motion, as I saw in the dim light, to slip it in his apron pocket first, but Miles reached out to intercept it. "Thank you, this will be on me." He smiled as he flipped open the folder to reveal, in addition to the waiter's paper pad and pen, a thin wallet I thought I recognized as my own. The waiter wheeled and made for the exit, but McDonald caught him by his apron strings. Pointing his pistol between the hapless man's shoulder blades, he echoed Miles's earlier question. "Now, sonny, do you have any change these men might have a right to expect?"

"No! You can't prove anything on me! Now, let me go!"

The tall man with the rifle bellowed, "We give you a ten-spot last night for our fifteen-cent suppers and our bar bill."

"It was a big bar bill," said the squirming waiter. "You bought for the house, as I recall."

"No argument there. But we was expectin' five bucks change and this is what we got." The man produced a piece of folded paper from his pants pocket.

McDonald seized it, unfolded it, and held it up to the light. "Why, this is fake as Mr. Pritchard's toupee there!"

"See, I told you!" said the gunman. Pritchard reached up to make sure of his hairpiece.

"Mr. Pritchard, why don't you pay these customers their due and let's send them on their way," instructed McDonald, who then turned to the intruders. "Get your weapons and put them away or I'll have to take all three of you in. Next time, you might call the law first before barging in and windin' up with somebody gettin' shot."

Deputy Garrigan offered to shepherd the waiter up to the marshal's office, but McDonald reminded him that counterfeiting was a federal offense, and he'd see to it the man was turned over to the proper authorities.

"You stay here and finish your story for Cap'n Miles," McDonald instructed before handcuffing the man and turning toward the door with him. "Maybe now you can help your boss appreciate the need for his assistance."

McDonald's admonishment seemed to have the desired effect on Garrigan's cooperation. The deputy holstered his firearm, awed. "Now, you were just talking about predicting the future or something like that," Garrigan said to Miles, "but how in blue blazes did you know those characters were about to come in the door?"

I was wondering the same thing myself, and wondered even more how my newfound companion had known that my wallet had been pinched.

"Not predicting the future—only foreseeing the likeliest consequences of what one has already seen of the past," said Miles smoothly. He went on to explain, "From my particular angle I observed, in the mirror behind the bar, the two men approaching the saloon door. The anger in their expressions was quite obvious. I did not take it for haste to be served the Ten-Cent Bratwurst & Beans Special, which was the only item chalked upon the menu board for today. I had also earlier witnessed the waiter casually drop a napkin beside Doctor Hooper there, and as Hooper was seated in my field of vision on the opposite side of the curved bench I could also infer, as the waiter bent to retrieve the napkin, that this had been a deliberate maneuver. I have watched some of the world's ablest pickpockets from Lahore to London, and I recognized the type.

"The full point of my argument, which I did not anticipate being demonstrated quite so dramatically just now, is that while it is not difficult to induce results forward from a circumstance, it is much harder, when presented with any particular event, to reason backward to the chain of smaller events that produced it. Deductive logic, in other words."

I for one was impressed. And from what I could observe of Miles's increased level of activity and speech, his still-tender wound must have been giving him some pain; although, in his apparent element of excitability as he took charge of the puzzling case, he appeared to me nervously animated.

"Well, you've convinced me," said Garrigan.

"Fine," Miles said. "Then may we have the rest of your story? Other tasks await us all, I'm sure."

The proprietor himself took that moment to interrupt with a tray of three brandies. "From my best bottle," he explained. "On the house."

Miles knocked his back, Garrigan sniffed and sipped, and I held my snifter between my palms and listened closely to the deputy's details.

"As I was saying, I walked around the body and took care not to touch or move it except to determine the man was dead for sure. I knew I'd need to fetch assistance, and I dashed outside to see who was about. Nothing. I checked around the shrubs in case the killer might be hiding; nothing again. It was nearly dawn, but the street was still empty except for one fellow."

"Who? Did you stop him?"

"No; it was only the lamplighter, who was up on the ladder dousing the oil lamp on the post in front of the house. I ran on around the corner toward the stable, and when I turned I could see he was moving on to the next lamppost with his ladder. I never saw another person—not so much as a dog—until I got to the livery and saddled my horse."

"You didn't question the man?"

"Didn't see any need to; I was in a hurry," Garrigan replied.

"What was he wearing, this lamplighter?"

"Jeez, I don't know. A brown vest and a gray shirt maybe? Dark trousers? Just like every other Tom, Dick, and Harry in town?"

"How about his hair color? Complexion? Height?"

"How could I tell? He was up a ladder and it was hardly light. Still sprinkling rain for that matter."

"Was he—a white man?"

"I didn't notice. I was in a hurry with a big case, I'm telling you."

"In so much of a hurry you may have . . . well, no matter now. Except one other thing I need to know before you go."

"What?"

"His shoes. Did you at least notice his shoes? Might he have been wearing leather moccasins?"

"Sorry, Cap'n. I don't have any recollection. But—wouldn't that have been a strange choice for a lamplighter?"

"Precisely, Garrigan. Precisely."

Chapter 5
A Corps of Allies

{In which Derrick Miles assembles his troops.}

THE LAWMAN TOOK HIS LEAVE OF US, and Miles pledged to be available at our Houston Street quarters once he'd discharged one crucial errand.

I followed him out into the blazing brightness of the street, which was made even more blinding by a heat that seemed to rise forcibly from the roadway in rippling waves. My Galveston hometown, I wagered in my mind, had nothing on Fort Worth for a humid July afternoon—and the city's notorious aroma of herds on hoof assaulted my sensibilities as well. I tried to smother the stench with my handkerchief.

"I've heard it called the smell of money, Hooper," said Miles, who turned confidently north as though he knew exactly where he was heading. It was on my mental list to go back to the camera shop and reclaim my equipment and prints, but I stuck with Miles as much out of curiosity as to ensure that he returned soon to Houston Street for essential rest.

"I believe I could prefer the poor house," said I before clapping the cotton square back over my nose.

Miles turned one block west and strode purposefully up the street, dodging wagons and drays, until he brought us to the door of the Western Union telegraph office on Main. He cocked his head to indicate I should accompany him inside. There I stood quietly by, hands clasped behind my back, trying not to eavesdrop, my eyes trained instead on a handbill posted on the wall. I took note that a ruffian by the ironic name of Davy Crockett was wanted for a trio of killings at the St. James Hotel up on the Cimarron.

"Can you take this message down?" I heard Miles whisper to the nearest clerk, a fresh-faced girl, to my surprise, in a uniform that looked a couple sizes too large for her frame. "And I am certain I may count on your discretion?" I myself continued to study the poster.

"Yessir, sir!" the young lady replied with verve, not softly. "You're my *first* customer."

"Ever?"

"My pa quit last week to go work on the railroad, but I've been learning the codes from him since I was a toddler. Boss Bundy hadn't had a wink of sleep, covering the wires all by himself. Except when his wife does the night shift. I've been training since Monday and got assigned to duty an hour ago."

"Well, then. Here we go," said Miles. "Begin with two-niner."

She took up her pencil and licked its sharpened tip. I turned back and pretended to study the bulletin board. "Ah . . . looking it up right now . . . that means—let's see—'Private, deliver in sealed envelope'?"

"Indeed. Then D as in dog, T as in Tom, mission done. Full stop." Miles waited for a long moment. "Read that much back, please?"

"D as in Dog, T as in—"

"No, just DT. I was clarifying the letters for you, which are of utmost importance."

"Oh! I've got it. DT mission done. Full stop."

"Full stop means the end of the sentence. You understand that?"

"Right, right," she replied. I glanced over my shoulder to see the girl flip her pencil end-up to apply a rubber eraser built right into the top. I marveled at the ingenious innovation as she made a quick amendment.

"Go on?" the young clerk said.

"G stop T stop T stop."

"Um . . . 'Gone To Texas'?"

"Bright one! Continue: Two-two-one B as in boy, Houston S as in Sam, T as in Tom comma, F as in father stop W as in whisky stop."

Tongue between her teeth, the girl penciled swiftly then looked up again. "221B Houston Street, Fort Worth. Is that all?"

"Await word stop. Miles—just as it sounds—then please end with niner-two."

"De—liver—promptly!" She finished up his message slip and read back over her handiwork, lips moving with her eyes as she scanned the text.

"Okay! Now, where would you like this addressed?"

"President U.S. Grant, The Capitol, Washington, D.C.," Miles replied evenly. I gave up all pretense of looking away. The clerk's pencil clattered to the floor. She gulped, then retrieved it.

"Yessir, sir. And—and to who do I make out the bill to?

"You mean, I assume, 'To whom do I make out the bill.' That would be Derrick Miles, Consulting Detective."

"All right, Mr. Detective. That'll be . . . two dollars and eighty-five cents. I'll—we'll send this to Washington right away, sir!"

Miles fished three trade-dollar coins from his vest pocket. "Thank you; you may keep the change. And what is your name, young lady? I may be needing your services again."

"Penny Whissell," replied the clerk. "Pleased to assist."

"Doctor Hooper," said Miles, turning to me, "it looks as though our business here is completed with Miss Whissell's help and we have made a valuable liaison in the bargain. I believe, for my part, a bit of rest is in order, and I shall return to our digs while you finish your own affairs."

I cleared my throat, which had gone dry as my mouth stood agape. "Your physician wholeheartedly approves of that plan. I shall, perhaps, see you again at the dinner hour?"

Miles nodded his assent, pulled his dark hat down to shade his eyes, and stepped back out into the steamy afternoon.

Young Penny Whissell's gaze followed him out the door. "Consulting detective? I've never heard of that!" she said.

"Neither had I, miss," I responded as I exited. "Neither had I."

The route to the camera shop at first eluded me, until I fell in with a clutch of rowdies making their way in the direction of something less tame than a spot of tea. I began to note familiar landmarks from yesterday's escapade—could it truly have been *yesterday?*—and soon relocated the establishment two doors down from the Standard Bar. I stepped into the shop vestibule which, reek though it might of nitric chemicals, was blessedly dark and cool. A bell tinkled as I shoved the door inward. I was suddenly very grateful to be back on the shady end of town, in either sense of the word.

I stepped to the counter and surrendered my claim check to the clerk on duty. He did not look like the man I'd seen the day before.

"Wait right here an' I'll get yer goods," he said. He wiped his hands on a black apron and disappeared behind a thick curtain. I waited, eyeing an ornate painted backdrop of a classical villa, in front of which were placed two side chairs, a potted plant upon a column, and a pair of wire-stand contraptions that I recognized as braces to hold a subject's head in place during an indoor portrait exposure. The canvas backdrop was frayed at the edges, the bentwood chairs dented and their cushions disgustingly stained by countless sitters.

It was six minutes, according to my watch, before the man returned with my camera kit. He set it upon the countertop but before releasing it asked my name.

"Hooper," I replied. "My information will be inside the case. Should you require it, I've written the serial number there on the claim check as well."

"That you have, m'boy, that you have. And a smart practice, too. You know, there's them as wouldn't be above swapping out for spare parts, if you get my meanin'." The fellow who'd called me "m'boy" seemed hardly of an age greater than my own, but his brassy deportment I judged to be a perfect match for the neighborhood. "We run an honest shop here, sir. I think you'll find everything in order—box and bellows cleaned, hinge oiled, lens covered, nameplate polished. *Doctor* Hooper, I see. And I have your prints here as well, with tissue laid in between for protection."

I tilted the cardboard mounts slightly, unable to resist a peek. The expected number of exposures were represented, and the quick glance I was able to steal in the afternoon shaft of light that cut through the gloom told me I'd had a very successful photographic outing. I let the lid float back down on the box and tucked the package under my arm. I paid up and left the clerk to his seedy studio and darkroom.

I coughed my way through ten more blocks of dust and haze as I trod up Main, almost to the river, before realizing that Houston Street must run parallel to my path on the west. Lot of good my Army orienteering course was doing me here in this godforsaken cowtown. If I was to make any sort of success here I'd certainly need a map. And next time, a hackney.

I relocated the doorway of 221 Houston at last. It was a well-proportioned entrance for all of its frontier construction; the door itself was of the style known in the South as cross-and-Bible, with stiles delineating the familiar shapes formed by six beveled panels, while a glazed demi-lunette above was divided severely by rails reminiscent of jail bars. It was painted black, and where a door knocker would ordinarily have been was mounted a heavy brass spur. I imagined it would make an announcement hard to ignore.

It was unlocked, for this was only the ground-floor entrance, which gave onto a basement access and a first-floor corridor, and beside that a stair to the second-story quarters I now called home for the moment. I walked up, set my camera and photos on a bench conveniently located beside the door, and inserted my newly acquired key into the lock as quietly as I could so as not to wake my co-lodger. I pulled off my boots and put them on the bench too.

In the small entry foyer Miles's hat was already hanging, and I set my own on a peg beside it. As I tiptoed past the dining table where only twenty-four hours earlier I had performed surgery, I spied an item that had not formerly been there. A large sheet of paper lay rolled up beside the magnifying glass I had seen Miles employ at the crime scene. I looked over toward the corner room I had coveted and found the door closed: a good sign. I breathed relief that my patient was indeed achieving a needed nap.

I pulled back an edge of the scroll. "A Bird's-Eye View of Fort Worth, Texas, 1876" read the cartouche in the lower corner. Intrigued, I spread the whole sheet out, though it sprang back partway into its cylindrical shape. I looked around for paperweights and realized that I had the perfect items already—my camera and case, which I retrieved from the hallway.

The map, elegant in its finely engraved detail, offered an astonishing representation of the regular street grid from the Trinity River at the north, to Elm Creek on the east and the environs of Hell's Half Acre on the southern fringe. Every building was represented in such detail that it was a simple matter to make out the exact spot on which I now stood. I could see why any detective would have found it an invaluable aid in understanding routes in and around the city, and Miles appeared to have examined it for that purpose. Finely penciled in were x's marking the brothel and its cribs we had visited on Rusk Street, and structures denoted in the legend as hotels and boarding houses—Fort Worth appeared to have some two dozen of them—were lightly circled. I took the opportunity to commit to memory the location of 221B Houston Street and other essential places before rolling the map back to its previous shape.

The room could do with a little fresh breeze, I decided, though it was hard to be sure whether the outside air would be an improvement. The generously upholstered chair beckoned suddenly. I felt the full weight of a short night and a long day. I sat. I slumped. I think I heard myself snore.

I dreamed—I believe—that I was aboard a locomotive steaming up and down the unpaved streets of Fort Worth, Texas. The train chugged on, picking up speed as it approached a creek with no bridge, its pistons laboring and knocking—

The knock, I realized with a start, was at the door.

"Come in?" I called out woozily as, still in my stocking feet, I tried to rise.

"You ordered supper?" called out a female voice behind me.

"No, I—how did you—"

Right behind the woman, a tall, thin figure in a cloak and odd-looking plaid cap swept in and relieved her of the heavy tray. It took a moment for me to recognize Miles in the shadows.

"Mrs. Simpson, we are truly obliged!" he said. He set the tray on the side table and moved to light the lamp.

"Thank you, dear. Captain Miles made all the arrangements for your meal, Doctor Hooper. He said you'd be starving. I am able to prepare some simple fare in my own kitchen—stew, sandwiches, the like—but your friend here said some restaurant specialties would be welcome. So I believe your steaks have been seared medium rare, your potatoes are buttered, and the bread is freshly baked," said our landlady.

I could not find fault with the arrangement, as the heavenly aroma sparked my appetite. I raised the window further to admit the cool night air, and thanked her for her thoughtfulness as Miles brought the tray over and she placed the delectable dishes at our two places.

"And he said to just add it to your bill, Doctor." Mrs. Simpson added. "Enjoy, now!"

She smiled and turned to leave but paused as another visitor arrived, signaling his presence with a purposeful knock on the open door.

Ranger McDonald brandished in his hand a folded newspaper. "Sorry for stoppin' by so late, fellows, but I did want to thank you for taking an interest in this case, Derrick. Turns out to be quite a puzzler, if I do say so. Right up your alley."

"Oh, the death of Councilman Daimmler, you must mean!" interjected Mrs. Simpson. "I read about it in the *Democrat* this afternoon. Are you two—"

"I do say, you have nothing to apologize for at all, Billy," Miles responded. "It is I who should thank you for bringing it to me. And yes, Mrs. Simpson, your tenants are indeed assisting the city marshal on the Daimmler case. I should have been more forthright with you about the nature of my work, but I hope you'll understand these matters often require a great deal of discretion, and besides, we did not yet know when we leased from you that we would be engaged on this one. May we count on your keeping things in confidence?"

Mrs. Simpson nodded dumbly as Miles continued, reaching over to take the paper from McDonald's hand. "If I were to wax philosophical," he said, "—and I do, on occasion, wouldn't you agree, gentlemen?—I'd venture that this Daimmler business challenges both the art and soul of detection. You've brought me a veritable study in crimson, Billy, a finely worked canvas whose layer upon layer of pigment represents the lifeblood of men and their motives. Looked at another way, there's the crimson thread of murder running through the colorless skein of life, and our duty is to unravel it, and isolate it, and expose every inch of it."

Bootless still, I pondered Miles's meaning.

Mrs. Simpson stared blankly at her lodger throughout the soliloquy.

McDonald, at last, spoke. "Couldn't have said it better myself."

Mrs. Simpson found her opportunity to exit, and Miles invited McDonald to pull up a chair and share our feast. He fetched a spare plate and utensils from the sideboard.

"I have to admit," McDonald said, "it beats the dickens out of those miserable beans at lunchtime."

Miles unfolded the paper to page one, shook his head, and turned the sheet around to show us its screamer headline: DEATH OF COUNCILMAN IN ACRE SHOCKS CITY. Something in the lower portion of the page caught my eye with a hint of familiarity, but before I could register more, Miles turned the page around again and shook it flat. He perused the lead story with growing chagrin and at last read aloud to us,

"'The Fort Worth Democrat has learned through well-placed city sources of the death early this morning of Mr. Ernst R. Daimmler, 56, under highly suspicious circumstances. A deputy marshal reported finding the deceased prone and fully clothed, alone in an abandoned house south of town, around five a.m.'

"'When Marshal Timothy Courtright arrived on the scene soon thereafter to conduct a thorough investigation, no cause of death could be immediately determined, nor was there any mark of violence discovered upon the body.'

"'There was, however, blood in abundance at the scene and, most dreadfully, employed to mark a foreign word upon the wall. Police are withholding information about exactly what the term was, though Courtright revealed that the name appeared to be that of a woman.'

"'The marshal's office continues to pursue the case as one of possible murder, although no suspect has yet been named. One Stengel, who is thought to be an associate, is being sought for questioning.'

"'The deceased was a widower, but a familiar figure in Fort Worth social circles and a member of its city council now serving his second term. Daimmler, in fact, had been among the party of officials attending the arrival of the Texas & Pacific Railroad on Wednesday and had offered one of the speeches on the occasion. A native of New Braunfels, Texas, Mr. Daimmler had come to Fort Worth with his wife in the city's early days, sometime around 1856, according to the best recollections of his colleagues. He was a freemason and a member of the Darmstadt Die Vierziger, a society of original German colonizers of Texas.'

"'Though holder of a ranching estate on the Clear Fork of the Trinity River east of the city, after the death of his wife five years ago, Mr. Daimmler maintained an address at a residential hotel on Calhoun Street, where he was last seen Wednesday afternoon. He has no other known relatives in the U.S., said a fellow council member who declined to be named for this story.'

"'Marshal Courtright, who was elected in June to the newly established office of Fort Worth city marshal by a margin of three votes, has called for increased law enforcement presence in all quarters, but especially in the den of vice known as Hell's Half Acre. He pointed to the present case as a prime example of the need for stronger protection measures.'"

Here, Miles paused and cleared his throat before resuming. "They've quoted the marshal: 'I am confident that with our vigorous pursuit of leads in the death of Mr. Daimmler, and the assistance of the Texas Rangers, we shall have a suspect in custody soon.'"

"Anything else?" I asked.

A wry half-smile passed across Miles's face. "'We assure the public that Mr. Courtright and his able deputy, Mr. Garrigan, are both engaged in the case and devoting a generous portion of their energies to it,' said Mayor

G. H. Day. 'We have complete confidence that these officers will nail down the facts and quickly get to the bottom of this heinous crime.'"

Miles slapped the paper down on his knee and burst out in a rueful laugh. "I told you, didn't I, that whatever happened, our city marshals would be sure to score?"

"That depends on how it turns out, doesn't it?" I replied. "Aren't you all pulling together, even if from different handholds on the rope?"

"Oh, don't be naïve. If the man is caught, it will be on account of their brilliant work; if he escapes, it will be in spite of it. It's heads I win and tails you lose. But I have yet to even inform you of my progress this afternoon."

"This afternoon?" I cried. "I thought you were resting and recovering your strength."

"Ah, my, Hooper, the detection of facts in a case that have escaped the notice of those in government employ is a most restorative tonic. Present company excluded, Billy," he interjected. "While you were engaged at the camera shop—as I see by your equipment here on the table—and enjoying your own siesta in the chair over there, I have set out my own agents to gather useful facts. I expect their arrival any minute now."

At the mention of the camera shop I recalled what had generated the spark in my cognition moments before. "Miles! Hand me that newspaper, if you would."

He passed it over, across McDonald's raised knife and fork, and I unfolded the sheet once more to reveal the next story below the lead. There, in precise graphical detail five columns wide, was a black-and-white engraving of the arrival of the T&P—from the perspective aboard the train that Miles and I had shared. Its particulars were exactly as I had observed them through my camera lens, right down to engineer Kelly's mindful stance and hand on the lever.

"Why—what the deuce—" I slammed the paper down, jumped up, and retrieved the box of eight-by-tens I had claimed that afternoon. I slid them partly out until arriving at the one showing the singular scene I had captured. That one I removed entirely from its wrapper and held up for Miles and McDonald to appreciate.

McDonald nodded and said, "Excellent work, Hooper! Congratulations on making the front page!"

Miles, however, broke out in a guffaw and slapped his knee. "*Now* who's incensed about others stealing the spotlight, my good doctor?!"

I could not contain my outrage. "The lousy thieves! They've copied my photograph and sold it to this upstart rag! My credit appears nowhere on this!" In a fit of pique that surprised even myself, I stood up, violently wadded the newspaper into a crumpled ball, and dashed it to the floor.

Miles continued, amused. "It's the nature of the beast, my friend. In whatever endeavor, we must be prepared to expose our brilliance to the appropriation of those slower on the draw. Or put another way, having feathered our nests patiently and expertly, we may arrive on any occasion to find that cuckoos have taken up residence. Now, may we set aside our irritations for the nonce and get down to the details of what evidence we have obtained so far?"

Chastened, I returned to my seat. McDonald and I cut into our steaks with gusto as Miles gave us an account of his discoveries.

"Hooper, it comes as a surprise to you that I was not resting within my chamber during a sweltering afternoon, because you assumed from the immediate signs that I had been here shortly before. That much is correct. I paid a visit to the printer's shop around the corner to have these made."

From his pocket he pulled out a stack of smartly engraved calling card for each of us. "And I also had the lucky discovery of this street map, which has helped tremendously in understanding the movements of persons about this city, which is not yet familiar to you and which has changed considerably since my last visit here. With the aid of it, I spent the remainder of the afternoon pursuing leads from this morning's clues—to useful advantage."

"How so?"

"In any city—even in our frontier outpost where the panther has only recently awakened—there is an assortment of eyes and ears that seem at first to be isolated, belonging to separate individuals; a casual glance from behind a curtain, a pair of feet crossing a street behind a wagon, a wave, a crooked finger, a traded penny. But these are in reality vital links in a network: a nearly invisible web of communication from alley to alley, rooftop to rooftop, fencepost to fencepost, among myriad figures whose names and faces are known to few. I am not speaking of any lodge or society, nor even of any organized underground, but of a loose confederation of boys too slippery for busy parents and grandparents to hold onto yet too young for gainful employment to be expected of them. They are not of the poorest classes, or they would be constrained in the workhouse or factory or farm;

nor are they of the rich, or they would have better delights than city streets at their disposal. Some are orphans; some, I admit, are truants, though I do not inquire too closely. They are shrewd, Hooper—keen observers of human habit, nimble, curious, and above all loyal to those who are able to appreciate their merits.

"To such an invisible army I would trust tasks no established police force could carry out without triggering alarm. People will let themselves be seen in circumstances, and overheard in conversations, that they never would in the presence of other adults—but around these urchins they let down their guard. I met with success today in recruiting a tribe of such locals for a reconnaissance mission."

"Oh?" asked McDonald. "And what would you have your tribe of urchins do?"

"They have already been about their task, Billy. Beginning at dusk I have had them tailing the informal corps of lamplighters as those figures emerge from the shadows to light. I estimate there to be only a dozen or so of these men employed in the city—and one of them knows something about this murder."

"How do you figure that?"

"Shortly after midnight Ernst Daimmler, city councilman, arrived by cab at a deserted apartment in the city's red light district. We may deduce the approximate time from the onset of a light rain, which had ended by the time the deputy marshal made his rounds at four. We know from his square-toed bootprints in the damp, packed soil of the street that Daimmler was the only passenger to alight there; I measured the shape and size of the print and confirmed that it matched those on the body."

"That makes excellent sense," said I. "But how did you come to know anything about another man—and to claim with such certainty how a murder was perpetrated?"

"I picked up a second set of prints in the dirt from a longer stride and a softer-style shoeprint—such as an Indian-style moccasin—going toward the cab, stopping there, and then keeping perfect pace with Square-toes as two wearers walked side by side up to the house; in the dust that coated the porch and hallway, the footsteps fell in line, with a pattern of water droplets alongside Moccasins. If it is raining, and this sequence of events occurs, what may we deduce, Hooper?

"Perhaps—perhaps Moccasins carried an umbrella!"

"Very good. And what might one surmise if one man meets another's conveyance, proffers an umbrella to protect him from a rain shower, and escorts him into the house?"

"That the men were previously acquainted . . . that the meeting was expected . . . and that Moccasins was taller than Square-toes," McDonald reasoned out.

"You'll make a fine lawman yet, Billy. It is possible, furthermore, to calculate with some precision the height of a person from the length of his stride when one is fortunate enough to be presented with a clear set of prints, and while you two and Courtright's goon were pawing over the dead body, I made many such observations and measurements. Now, the discovery of the brothel token was another stroke of good fortune, and you may be certain that Courtright and Garrigan have been abroad today questioning every whorehouse owner and patron in the city."

"And you have not?" I asked.

"I found only one call necessary," Miles replied. "Though I took pains to change my costume before making it. This newfangled Scottish hunting cap with brims fore and aft also has flaps that can be tied with a ribbon at the crown, or alternately unfastened to cover one's ears. A handy disguise, no? And much less unwieldy than a sombrero."

He continued, "Determining to stop in at the Rusk Street lodgings of one Ophelia Dixon"—I glanced over to see if my companion was making a jest, but he proceeded with a straight face—"I turned up some useful information. The now retired Madam Dixon happens to have been the mentor of a notorious figure recently arrived at the Flats over at Fort Griffin, and of other protégées throughout the frontier."

"Big Nose Kate," said McDonald. "Brought her trade to Texas from St. Louis, as I understand it."

"And if any woman possesses the wit to glean a man's secrets in order to use them at the most opportune moment, it's Kate, and I believe she learned from the best. Upon visiting Madam Ophelia I gained one critical fact: that there is no, ahem, sporting woman currently working in Fort Worth, Texas, who goes by the name Rachel. The metal token, I surmise, is a signal."

I nodded silently, digesting this conclusion and swallowing another bite of the juicy tenderloin.

"I have a theory about the reason for the rendezvous as well." Miles was in the midst of explaining when a sound of scuffling feet arose in the stairwell. A catchy seven-beat rhythm was tapped out against the door, and Miles stood to answer it.

"Ah, here are our able agents now!" he said.

Miles opened the door to admit half a dozen of the scruffiest, noisiest, most mannerless bunch of ragtag youths I had ever encountered. They seemed to tumble through the doorway all at once, like lumps of coal being dumped from a chute. One, thin and of middling height, perhaps a year older than the others, appeared to be the leader of the pack.

"We done just like you said, Cap'n!" he cried out excitably. The boy's eyes followed his nose to the cutlery and bare meat bones strewn across our dinner plates—and the others jostled to see what he was looking at.

"Then remember what else I instructed, men," Miles said to the scattered group. "Discipline and discretion, all. Line up over here and allow me to introduce you."

The older boy cocked his head as a signal for the others to settle in. The teeming mass of youngsters quieted and sorted themselves quickly into an orderly row. I marveled at the transformation.

"Colleagues, meet the Panther Cubs. Recently recruited to assist as required. We shall receive a report from their top cat, Tolliver here. But first I want to assure you that these youths have pledged their loyalty to me—and to upholding the law. When they are in my employ they will be dependable and stay out of trouble." Turning to the company of Cubs, Miles added, "Do these gentlemen have your word?"

All nodded assent.

"Very good then. Tolliver, tell me, and Doctor Hooper, and Officer McDonald, what you have learned."

"Well, we did just like you said, Cap'n—we all lounged about till dusk, then we spread out around the city and each picked our man. One o' the guys who lights the street lanterns. They're easy to spot carryin' those ladders around. We covered every neighborhood that has street lights—you said we was s'posed to follow 'em quietly and see where they went after their work was done."

"Indeed. Go on."

"Well, four of 'em went home to houses. We got addresses for you. Buster here followed one man to the stables, where he hung up his ladder and headed off on a horse. Five others took off for the tavern on Tenth. But the fellow I myself tailed, down in the Acre, carried his ladder all the way back uptown to a hotel—like you asked about—and stowed it in the alley at the back. I did wonder, why's a lamplighter living high on the hog in a hotel? Not that it was all fancy or anything. The Pickwick, you know the place, on Throckmorton Street? Well, I slipped in the front and told the doorman I was supposed to wait for my pop to come back from the opera house. I heard the mark ask, 'Has Mr. Stengel returned?'"

"Stengel, you say? That is a useful bit of information."

"Funny thing, though—when the clerk said no, the gent paused for a minute—seemed kind of undecided—and then left again. He walked across the street, curled up on a park bench, and fell fast asleep! That's where I left him, to come here."

"Good work, lad, good work. Now—I trust you can all get a meal and some sleep yourselves. Tomorrow before dawn, Tolliver, do you think you can find this same lamplighter again? Bring me word of his actions when you do. Be discreet."

"Discreet, Cap'n?"

"Keep mum about any of this."

"Oh, right!"

"We are close to answers—very close!" declared Miles. "Here's a quarter for each of you, until needed again. Knock on Mrs. Simpson's door downstairs, and she'll have hot sandwiches packed and ready for all. Dis-*missed!*"

The boys took their two-bit pieces with amazement and scattered into oblivion, swiftly but much more quietly than they had arrived.

McDonald observed before standing to take leave himself, "Damnation, Derrick—if I don't start to appreciate why you were made the youngest brevet officer in Grant's army!"

Miles shrugged. I filed away that surprising bit of information as we bid our guest good-bye.

One more task remained before I retired for a longer night's rest: to check my patient's sutures and change the dressing on his shoulder. We cleared the dinner dishes from the table and again placed a sheet across it. He lay face down upon it.

I was pleased to note that throughout a full day's exertions not a stitch had loosened, and the redness around the bullet wound was retreating nicely.

I repeated application of the salve Miles provided, as he told me more about what he had gathered during his audience with Madam Dixon that afternoon. I tried to follow his conversation as he flattened out his shoulders and pointed his chin floorward.

"Ophelia's not an obvious source of information to an East Texas arriviste like Courtright," he explained, "though she may be the most valuable one in all of Fort Worth. You may well think ill of my admitting to any association, but it's not what you might guess."

"I am beginning to understand that is frequently the case with you."

"I spent some of my formative early adolescence at Griffin, when the fort was established after the War between the States. You can imagine the sort of temptations and troubles a place like that might present to a thirteen-year-old."

"Indeed . . . not too different, I suppose, from those brought with them by camp followers throughout the war, when I was too busy patching up wounded boys in blue to notice."

"The fascinations of the Flat provided an effective sanctuary for dodging the lash of my so-called guardian and his wife. But Madam Ophelia saw to it that none of her fancy girls ever considered me game. She watched over me like a mother hawk—like the mother I never knew when my father left her behind in merry olde England."

"Your parents were British?"

"Let's step back a few years. One Percival Woodrow Miles was a Lincolnshire mapmaker with a romantic interest in westward exploration and, particularly, admiration for the leaders who established a new republic on the North American continent and the breakaway Texians who had defended the Alamo. Mr. Miles made his fortune in surveying enterprises for railways across the British Isles, while dreaming of emigrating to the West, especially when Texas joined the Union in 1845 and new lands opened up for American rails. His wife, who was busy raising their young son, did not share his interests.

"By 1852, though, the lure was irresistible. That year my father, recruited by the empresarios of a colony on the Texas frontier to settle a boundary dispute, jumped at their offer. He sailed for the States and left his wife and son behind."

"What an awful thing to do to you!" I blurted out.

"Not me; that would be my older brother. I came along two years after, the product of an unsanctified alliance between surveyor Miles and a part-Kiowa servant at Fort Belknap."

Now I really had put my foot in it. I remained silent as I attended to re-dressing the wound site on Miles's shoulder.

"Enough of my origins," he said, raising his chin while I applied gauze. "Suffice it to say, when war broke out in 1860 my father left me behind in the care of the quondam Texas Rangers just as he had abandoned his first wife and child. But I suppose I found the frontier a more rigorous, maybe more rewarding, schooling than if I had boarded at Eton. The experience opened some important doors. Most of all to old Sam Houston himself—the man who had inspired my middle name and seven years ago provided a letter of introduction that eventually got me to Washington and London. . . . and out of those miserable forts. I may have left the place behind, Hooper, but the lessons, I have always carried with me. In due time, when I returned to America, I served my reunited country during the recent Red River campaigns—but I never saw my father again."

"Excuse my presumptions, then, Captain," I said with what I hoped came off as lighthearted sincerity. "You were saying, about your audience with Madam Ophelia?"

"Yes. Ernst Daimmler, she explained, oversaw a clandestine society known as the Rächer. The Avengers. Few appreciate the full extent of this organization's murky activities, and not even Ophelia could enlighten me much on that score, but the association has roots going back for decades on the frontier, to an earlier, more violent era of white settlement. And she revealed that Daimmler was tight with a half-breed mercenary known as Stinger, who does the bidding of this group. We find Stinger—and I wager we've found our murderer."

"The lamplighter, then?"

"That's one possibility."

"How many others are there?"

"Oh, I'll know our man when we see him. Of that there can be no question."

The examination completed, Miles sat up on the table, still shirtless, and reached into his trousers pocket, bringing out a tidy envelope half an inch thick. I was caught staring, looking over the man's slim, taut frame and nearly hairless chest, cogitating on how one of his obvious youth had come to attain a position of high responsibility in military service. Of his ability to persuade others to his bidding, however, and of his keen faculties as a strategist, I had set aside any doubt.

"I haven't failed to note that I owe you for services rendered," said he, placing the packet in my hand. "Tell me if it isn't sufficient. Nor would I have you think me a freeloader. Among this afternoon's numerous errands was a stop at the bank. You'll find my share of July's room and board, and an advance on August."

"Oh, I never thought—"

"Yes, you did, and this should put your mind at ease."

"But the medical treatment, really, there's no need. We'll be square if you'll simply tell me how you came to know of this miracle ointment!"

Miles half-laughed. "Spend time among the Indians, and you will learn many interesting and useful things," he said. "Spend time with me, and I shall tell you more."

The youngest captain in Grant's army changed into his dressing-gown, settled into the armchair beside the open window, and took up the violin he had left on the side table. I took my candlestand up the stairs and prepared for a more restful night. From my bed in the storey above I listened, my eyelids becoming heavy but sleep eluding me, as the tunes moved from "Fox on the Run" to "'Tis Not True" to "Hangèd Shall I Be."

I pondered on the long day's events and wondered what the next would bring.

Chapter 6
COURTRIGHT IS ALMOST RIGHT

{In which details come to light.}

THE SUMMER SUN WOKE ME, shining through my lone window, and I rose swiftly, fearing the day already well advanced before checking my watch with relief. I washed up, and had finished combing my hair and arranging my shirt collar and new-fashioned bow tie when I heard a knock downstairs and the voice of Miles at the door.

"Good morning, Miles! A word, if you have time." The voice belonged to our fresh acquaintance Jim Courtright. I hastened down the steps into the parlor, where the marshal was removing his hat.

"What sort of news brings you here before seven, sir?" asked Miles, still in his dressing gown.

"Nothing less than the identity and motive of a murderer. All in a day's work."

"Well," said Miles, turning in my direction and arching an eyebrow, "If you've solved a crime with such alacrity, what need did you have to come calling for further advice?"

"Oh, none whatsoever—we already have one man under lock and key, I assure you. I only stopped by to tender your fee."

"Did you hear that, Hooper! Why, it was only last evening we were enjoying a repast in this very room and reading in the papers of just such a prediction."

"Oh, indeed," I said, as I stepped off the bottom stair and walked over to shake the lawman's hand. "Come, sit, and I shall put on a pot of coffee while you fill us in on the details. That is, of course, if you can spare a moment."

"No need to worry about the coffee, Hooper," said Miles. "You'll find it brewed and sitting on the stove."

Courtright had already slid into the armchair that I had begun to think of as mine. "Don't mind if I do, while Garrigan and the boys round up our suspect."

Miles took the opposite armchair, upon which with no mistaking he had already laid his regular claim, and I went to pour cups for myself and our impromptu guest.

"I'm happy to take a moment's ease for a stretch," said Courtright. "It's a wearying business, maintaining law and order and bringing criminals to justice." He leaned back and ran his fingers through his blond locks. "Not so much the physical exertion, really, but the sort of mental exhaustion that fellows like you and I experience, Miles. Cracks the noggin to put the intellectual faculties to work as incessantly as the two of us do, doesn't it?"

"I imagine the strain must be considerable," Miles commented.

I handed the marshal a coffee in one of Mrs. Simpson's dainty china cups and implored him to tell us the name of the suspect he had arrested. Miles sat up straight with a look of rapt attention—and dare I say, worry?—apparent in his features.

"It'll be quite the scandal when it gets out, I assure you. The fellow in the calaboose for the murder of Ernst Daimmler is none other than John Smith, a onetime clerk in Daimmler's employ who it turns out was running a numbers racket out of the back of Mrs. Love's establishment."

Miles stood and walked to the window, clapping his hands together. "I suppose congratulations are in order for your brilliant work. Can you reveal to us how you came to this conclusion?"

"Like I said, it required some brain-busting. But don't fret, I'll pay you anyway. You did help us in the details about the cab. He reached into his breast pocket and pulled out an envelope, which he patted absentmindedly against his other palm as he continued. "So, as soon as our little group parted company yesterday, I paid a call to Mrs. Love, who owns the house and a nearby row of female dormitories, including the one where the victim was found. I showed her the token we had taken into evidence, and although she said that no Rachel had been in her employ for some years, coincidentally a caller had visited on Tuesday inquiring, without success, for just such a girl.

"I then interviewed each of the councilmen and learned that Daimmler had sent his assistant packing the previous Friday. Councilman Brown let on that he suspected Smith was putting the squeeze on Daimmler."

Miles appeared to be digesting all of these details calmly as he sipped his coffee. "Go on."

"I checked in with a lawyer buddy who said the guy was born Johannes Schmidt back in Bavaria. Daimmler was apparently the man to see in these parts if you were looking to relocate from the Old Country and leave a questionable record behind."

"I had learned as much myself from a patron at the biergarten on Main last evening," said Miles. "So how did you connect Smith with the crime?"

"Well, sir, here's the other thing Mrs. Love told me when I returned and informed her of the reason for my investigation. She was shocked when she heard a killing had taken place at one of her properties—and not because there'd been a death, mind you, but because she hadn't already known about it first. Plenty of crimes of passion happen in the Acre, and don't lack for witnesses. But this one was thought through. Calculated. And it didn't involve any of the madam's girls."

Miles was about to pose another question when an urgent knock sounded at the door, interrupting him.

I hurried over and turned the knob, and in stumbled the youth who went by Tolliver. None of the other Panther Cubs were in evidence.

"Cap'n! You've got to come quick! Your man Stengel is back, and it looks like he might have company!"

Miles was on his feet in a flash and reaching for his hat— not the Western one but the newly acquired deerstalker. He reached into his pack, which had been hanging on the coat hook, to transfer a couple of small items to his pocket. One, I was certain, was a gun.

"We'd better follow their lead, Marshal, if you want to nab your suspect."

"A little early in the day for him to show up at Dollie Love's, don't you imagine?"

"You wait till tonight, and your man'll be long gone," Miles shot back. He pulled on his cloak and reached into its pocket. "Here's a dollar, Tolliver. Go hail us a hack, quick."

But before the youngster could turn around, a sound erupted of boots taking the stairs two at a time. Into the room burst Deputy Garrigan.

"Marshal Courtright—" he gasped, "we've got Schmidt in the lockup. But the witness you had me tailing, that Stengel?"

"What, Garrigan? Spit it out!"

"He's turned up dead."

Among the motley company descending on the Pickwick Hotel, I for one was silently grateful that our newly adopted frontier city had fostered a readily available network of hackney cabs: our hired driver seemed to dispatch four of us as speedily as a single cannon shot to our destination six blocks away, without the need to locate the livery and saddle up individual horses, or hoof it on the hot sidewalk. A hanger-on in this erupting detective business, I would have been hard pressed to keep pace with better riders—but would fain have begged off accompanying them, as I sought to keep an eye on my recovering patient. I kept my medical kit handy just in case.

None would have guessed, from the agility with which Derrick Miles sprang from the cab onto the hotel's plank sidewalk, the injury he'd endured so recently.

Nor must the manager of the Pickwick have anticipated such a party pouring into his lobby: the badge-waving city marshal, accompanied by his pistol-packing goon, a tall man in a hunting cap, and a puzzled doctor with his medical bag, struggling to keep up with the procession. A ragtag army of guttersnipes on foot could not have been far behind.

The frazzled desk clerk pointed down the hallway to a back door. "Out back in the courtyard. Your man Crow's there, Marshal."

As Garrigan had explained during our short, bone-rattling cab ride, the victim's lifeless and twisted body had been discovered, prone and entangled in the rung of a wooden ladder, upon the bricks of the hotel's tree-lined and partly fenced patio some ten feet below the open hotel window and ten feet out from the wall. The dead man, of middle age, long dark hair, and tanned, reddish complexion, was in shirtsleeves, vest, and brown cotton trousers—and wore soft, Indian-style moccasins. The distraught guest who had come upon the scene while heading out for a morning cigar had been in the midst of reporting the incident to the clerk at the moment Garrigan and Crow were arriving, too late, to arrest their second suspect. He identified the prone man as a fellow lodger he'd seen in the corridors, and the clerk had him down as a Mr. Stengel.

While Courtright and Garrigan made straight for the courtyard, Miles cocked his head to indicate I should follow him up the inside staircase.

I must have shot him a quizzical look, but he held a finger to his lips and continued to the second floor. I wondered what folly I had gotten myself into . . . but I followed. He turned a few steps down the hallway and stopped in front of Room 208. Quietly he turned the knob, which yielded. He had drawn his pistol as he all at once opened the door into the room.

No threat immediately presented itself, but the sitting area was a shambles. There appeared to have been a struggle. And across the bedroom wallpaper was daubed in red a word already familiar to us from the previous morning: *R A C H E.*

Miles walked around the perimeter of the scene, so as not to disturb footprints that carried traces of blood as well as red dirt. Some were obviously made by a hard-soled boot, others by softer footwear.

On the bedside table sat a clear, capped vial a quarter-way full of white powder. Miles left it there.

I watched in astonishment as the self-proclaimed consulting detective calmly followed the track of boot prints from the table, to the wall where the message was still freshly wet, and then, in a swift, fluid step, to the door of a tall armoire, which he flung open.

A desperate, startled gasp escaped from the figure hiding therein, behind a gabardine jacket that was insufficient to provide much cover.

"Step out slowly," Miles directed, keeping the gun aimed steadily, "and let the doctor here tend to your injury. We know you are innocent of murder. We do not, however, know your name."

"P-Plummer, sir. J-Jack Plummer."

"Hooper, if you'd be so kind as to help this gentleman down from his perch and find out where he's bleeding? I'll summon the others."

Miles walked to the tall open window, still taking care to leave the scene undisturbed, and leaned out. "If you fellows are done cuffing your stiff there, come on up and let's hear a few facts from an eyewitness," he shouted down.

The unfortunate Mr. Plummer had suffered the deep slash of a knife to his upper arm, I discovered after instructing him to be seated on the bed. He had done his best to stanch the bleeding with a cheap towel and his necktie, but it was an awkward job for him to have attempted one-handed.

As I held the man's injured arm, examining it, a pair of handcuffs appeared from Miles's cloak pocket as though out of thin air, and before either the suspect or I could register a word, Plummer found his good hand secured to the iron bedframe.

"A precaution against any risk of flight until we establish some facts," Miles said. Plummer's face registered surprise, but he did not resist.

I replaced the man's makeshift tourniquet with a rubber one, administered a whiff of smelling salts, and got down to work cleaning the wound while Miles kept the man preoccupied with questions. I could only wish for some of the carbolic acid I'd used on Miles' own injury, with the technique he'd so recently taught me.

"Plummer, you say. The name calls to mind some familiarity in the annals of Texas," said Miles.

"That could be," the man replied through clenched teeth. He was young, perhaps of an age with Miles himself, and of average build. His hair and neat beard were a sandy brown and his clothes fashionable but not flashy. Other than the disheveling effects of a scuffle—with Stengel, I assumed—he seemed the type to take care with appearances.

I was in the process of instructing him to hold the cloth with the salts over his face as I made what I hoped were swift sutures, when the three lawmen entered, with Tolliver trailing them and sneaking in behind. Plummer, pale-faced and sweating, shut his eyes and held his breath.

"Marshal, meet Jack Plummer, who's about to enlighten us on a few facts of this bloody case as soon as my colleague can bandage him up," said Miles. "You might as well find a place to sit, but steer clear of the evidence, would you?"

Tolliver piped up. "It's 'im, the lamplighter I was tailin'!"

"And for that valuable bit of evidence we are appreciative, I assure you," Miles said.

Courtright did not appear so grateful. "How can you be so certain this man here isn't a double murderer? We've got a body growing cold downstairs in the laundry room that he might need to answer for."

"All in due time, men, all in due time. I am hoping Mr. Plummer will fill in the gaps."

Plummer released a deep sigh as I knotted and trimmed the catgut and wrapped his arm with clean gauze. I unbound the tourniquet slowly and watched as his complexion and breathing started to return to normal. He would be in considerable discomfort for a few days, but I was at least

convinced that his blood loss had not been severe. The cut had been clean—
from a finely honed edge—and glancing rather than stabbing in nature. Both
circumstances boded well for full healing.

The patient dabbed his brow with a handkerchief and sized up the group
in the room before saying more. "Thank you for recognizing my innocence,
whoever you are," he said to Miles. "Though I feel I've been dragged into
some unsavory business and would be glad to lay it out for you. I had a sense
that Stengel was bad news, but if he's dead it's his own doing—and I can
bear eyewitness to how he did away with Mr. Daimmler."

"Oh, he's dead, of that you can be sure," said Garrigan, his Irish brogue
turning the syllable to *shurr.*

"These men represent the law in these parts and will be glad to hear
your story," Miles added, then introduced himself and the occupants lining
the perimeter of the stuffy room, coming around to me. "And you're lucky
Doctor Franklin Hooper here was on hand. I can testify to the efficacy of
his work."

Plummer, regaining his color somewhat, settled back against the head-
board. "Well, thanks for that, too."

"Now, Tolliver—if you're going to lurk, make yourself useful and fetch
some water and drinking glasses for these folks, would you?" Miles instructed.
"And let the manager know he needn't send the chambermaid just yet, but
we could use a few of his dining chairs."

"The telling might take a while, gentlemen," Plummer said, exhaling.
"The story's a sordid one, and long, I'm afraid. I believe you'll understand
better if I start way back—before the beginning."

"Plunge in, Mr. Plummer. We have time. Don't we, Marshal Courtright?"

Part II

IN THE COUNTRY OF THE PEOPLE

{A Tragedy of Old Tejas}

Chapter 7
TWO SEEDS

{In which peoples are set one against the other.}

FOR COUNTLESS SEASONS THEY HAD DOMINATED this vast land that belonged to no one and everyone equally. They called themselves the Numunuu, for after they had defeated every enemy tribe in battle and rendered them all inconsequential they had earned the right to be known simply as the People. Perhaps every band of conquerors on the earth designated themselves thus in their own tongue, considering those they had vanquished but a cipher, a nonentity; about such a possibility the Numunuu gave no thought. To themselves, which is all that mattered, they were the People.

But their enemies, pushed back to the edges of the vast buffalo plains, had a different name for them, and the People had gotten wind of it: *Comanche,* Those Who Make War Against Everyone. The People knew also of the name they were called by the taibo, the more vexing population of light-skinned newcomers who had begun arriving from the direction of morning: Lords of the Plains. The People snorted derisively when they learned of this, for it was a name that could have been bestowed only by a pathetic race accustomed to being ruled, who had been long subjugated as vassals themselves by masters in lands across the great sea.

The People had grasped some of the interlopers' tongues, and traditions, and tools. They gained insight first from the agents of the great lord of España, who had conveniently killed off many of the People's own enemies from south across the desert and across the great river the Spanish now called Rio del Norte.

In the language of the taibo the People were called Indio. What a laugh the medicine man had who first heard this; his story spread as fast as camp smoke through band after band across generations and became more amusing with the retelling. That the taibo, upon first arriving on this land's shore, thought they had traveled all the way across the ocean and had come almost around to where they started—like a dog that had chased its own tail and, encountering it, exclaimed that he had found a new mate.

That these first emissaries of the white taibo mistook the People for a different group and called them Los Indios did not bother them. Most of Lord España's men probably did not know *taibo*—list-checkers—was the name the Numunuu called them, either. What did bother the People was anyone attempting to settle down within their domain. That meant trouble. And with every passing moon it was happening more often. With the arrival of each summer there were more strangers, by now enough to pose a distinct threat.

Other new languages from the rising sun, with words like *das Gesetz* and *das Recht* and *mein* and *treaty* and *own*, soon sounded on tongues within hearing of the People. These unmelodic words crept up to the Plains from the south and east like plagues or storms. During powwows and councils the elders spoke quietly, then more stridently, of these arrivals.

The newcomers' manner of believing they could lay claim to earth herself, to the very mother ground that sustained all life, at first puzzled and then disturbed the People. What had been open to all humankind, the taibo had closed.

Worse, the newcomers had brought fire from long poles — deadly fire.

The People had been successful in halting such intrusive activity from the far south by aggressively taking captives, eliminating them or enslaving them as seemed prudent. Lord España had finally understood and left them alone. Lord England and his friends, though, kept coming. Parleys and councils and treaties—the Europeans' words now known with unease to the People— yielded only hollow promises.

Now these interlopers must be stopped, and the People knew how.

The vassals of Lord España, centuries earlier, had been useful to the People in trade and as slaves. And from the Spanish, the People also had taken their greatest prize of all: the horse.

Tuhuya, the People called this four-legged beast. It was not as tall as the native animal that provided their sustenance, the tasiwóom which thundered across the plains in enormous, unstoppable waves and were hunted by the People for food, clothing, and shelter. It was not shaggy. Its flesh was not palatable; its hide was not malleable. But where the bison thrived by brute force and bulk and their reliance on the herd to protect themselves, the unhorned, unbearded horse survived by speed, agility, and cunning. Those traits, as the People learned from the Spanish invaders, could be tamed and used.

The People had watched the Spaniards of old blow into the nostrils of young horses to calm them, as they whispered and brought them around to do their bidding. Once the People learned to mount, and to hunt mounted, they also found they could fight mounted, and furthermore—free of the metal clothing and other encumbrances of the men with iron fire—better. On horseback, the People grew faster, and with each new generation, more masterful.

Southward with the summer season the People sought the bison, which had come seeking grass. Inevitably this migration brought them within sight of cookfires among dugout houses and log cabins, and within the startling view of fields cleared of trees and grass, where the cultivation of food crops had begun. Fences and fortifications had been built. Unless severe action were taken, no longer would the bison roam free across the buffalo plains. The livelihood and lifeways of the People were at risk.

Destruction and enslavement would teach the white men, just as these strategies had taught their old enemies the Spaniards. The People would take revenge. They would take captives.

Coming to the margin of the Navasota River, so called for clay pots made from the mud of the Brazos Valley that was also an ancient killing field of bison and other wildlife, were a white tribe from the far north. Down from the Wabash farmlands of Illinois, where they'd first settled, across the Ozarks and Ouachitas they arrived by wagon, removing to the green prairies of what Lord México—now split from Lord España across the ocean—called Coahulia y Tejas.

The tribe brought with them oxen and iron and woolens and tools and guns, and a brand of religious thought founded on the exclusion from their Christian heaven of anyone unlike them. For the predestinarian Baptists of the Parker clan, the hereafter was reserved for the elect of the chosen white races, the good seed of Adam. Those born instead from the wicked seed of the serpent were doomed already to eternal punishment. They were beyond redemption, not only unworthy of, but immune to, the gospel of salvation.

So when the patriarch Elder John Parker and his wife, Patsey, and their children and grandchildren and a handful of other kin and allies, including the Plummers and the Dutys, made the journey overland in the year of their lord 1833 from the Illinois grubstake that had for a short time been their home, to the frontier of Texas, they settled not only on the fertile banks of the Navasota but within the hunting range of the People.

They settled in the beating heart of Comanchería.

Chapter 8
MORNING IN MAY

{In which lambs are caught and slaughtered.}

IN THE MONTH OF THE FLOWER MOON in the year the taibo list-makers numbered as 1836, the People plotted a mission to stop the encroachment of the white settlers who had come to the buffalo lands they hunted.

The council enumerated its complaints: The settlers felled trees and dammed streams. When they made promises in trade exchanges, they failed to keep their word. They held no councils, answered to no chief. They built fortified tipis that looked as though they meant to stay. If the People did not make war on these taibo, the chiefs reasoned, the taibo would soon make war on them. The settlers would drive them from the plains.

The People knew this from other red nations. Traders brought news of the wretched Cherokees, who feared they might be forced from the mother land of tall trees and tall mountains. Already the Great Father of the taibo had ruled: "No purchase, grant, lease, or other conveyance of land, or of any title or claim thereto, from any Indian nation or tribe of Indians, shall be of any validity in law or equity . . . ." If the People could make no sense of such terms, they nonetheless understood well their effect.

By agreement none of the People would tell the taibo, or even their own allies, which of their war chiefs planned the mission. They would never reveal who took part. They would face retribution equally, and without faint-heartedness. For there was always retribution, and retribution for retribution.

Inside the Fort Parker stockade that bright Thursday morning, three generations of women went about their chores in their several households. James Parker's wife, Martha, and Silas's wife, Lucinda, along with Lucinda's sister Elizabeth, managed things, despite the seniority of old Granny Parker.

In their cabins they set the cleaned-up breakfast dishes high on rude shelves supported by pegs between the chinked logs. They made beds, then swept clear the dirt floors that had been disturbed during dressing, mealtime activity, and morning prayers. They hung aprons back on single wooden pegs. They banked cookfires in the fieldstone hearths and swung pothooks back out of the way, for this glorious May day would be one for work out of doors in the fields, far outside the tall stockade fence.

Elder John and his grown sons Silas and Benjamin were already hoeing in the furrows, and the bigger children would soon be expected to join them. Farm work constituted as vital a component of the youngsters' education as learning to read the holy scriptures, or mastering mathematics, or carpentry, or sewing. The family's sustenance came from the ground as much as it did from the wild game taken in the forests or the beef, milk, and mutton husbanded within their fenced grazing lands.

The men handled the most challenging tasks of the communal farm, such as hoeing and ox-plowing, as their height and strength were advantages. In addition to the precious metal-headed tools they employed, they kept their firearms near at hand. Wild animals posed one threat, the red man a more serious one. Some of the Parker menfolk had lately helped organize a militia called the Rangers, who had struck out against area Indians to forestall attacks, punish offenders, and to prove the settlers' intent to stay.

The Parkers and their kin were not unaware they had chosen a dangerous place. They had come to the frontier as a calculated calling—to establish their Protestant church in advance of any prohibition from Catholic Mexico City, and as a bulwark against continued incursions of the Indians into populated colonies. Now no longer Texians but newly made Texans after Sam Houston's victorious battle at San Jacinto, the Parker clan had returned to their fort on the Navasota the previous week rejoicing and ready to redouble their labors, but wary of yet another worry.

News of Indian raids on frontier homesteads traveled swiftly by word of mouth. Gory, detailed accounts of abductions spread through the frontier newspapers and were often read aloud in meetinghouses and parlors as lighted lanterns and flickering firelight cast the world outside unglassed windows into creeping, terrifying shadows. But the Parkers knew the Lord was on their side. They determined to press on with the aim of claiming the land for a young nation and a Christian God. It was their holy duty. They must tame and till the land, and continue to populate it with the sanctified progeny of Adam.

On Wednesday night all the community had slept restively inside the fort, except three able men: Sarah Parker's husband, Lorenzo Nixon; Rachel Parker's husband, Luther Plummer; and the Parker sisters' father, James, who had gone to tend a field a mile away and camped overnight there. Word had come that the tribes planned a raid. But the patriarch's son Silas—who along with James had hewn the logs and hoisted the palisades and thatch by dint of their own sweat and purses the previous spring on tracts granted for their military service—was resolute. No scattered mob of misfit red men, the unwashed and unworthy, would stand against their fortifications. For they were doing the Lord's work.

Not long after sunup, as was forewarned, the savages appeared. A great and fearsome horde of them, hundreds, on horseback. The Indians made as though to parley under a white flag. Benjamin Parker, eldest of the patriarch's sons, knew not to trust it. But perhaps he could buy time for the others. *Run,* he whispered to the women and children before striding out to the false banner and his doom.

Rachel, several months pregnant with Luther's second child, stood transfixed at the half-open gates of the fort, struck speechless by the numbers of natives that had appeared as suddenly as crows among the cornrows. She could think only of birds, evil omens. Like the flight of hundreds of starlings the savages had silently emerged from the trees, formed themselves into a mass movement, and then burst out into raucous, menacing activity. One moment the pastoral scenery was clear of any threat; the next it was a hopelessly one-sided crisis.

"Run little Rachel, for your life and your unborn child, run now and fast!" she heard her uncle Benjamin bark at her before she decided she would heed his advice and make for the woods where, maybe, her father and her husband would shield and save her. Benjamin strode forward through the gates to confront the enemy. Rachel fled out the back.

But weighed down by the baby in her womb as well as a not-yet-two-year-old barely walking, she was not as swift as the others. The invaders caught up with her and the toddler and swept them up behind riders, just as they did feeble Granny Parker and the resourceful Elizabeth Kellogg, who had nonetheless lost valuable time while digging up the coins that were the clan's savings.

Captured too were Cynthia Ann and John, the two young children of Silas and Lucinda Parker—children already rendered fatherless in that moment as Silas stubbornly made his bootless stand. Girl and boy would both be of an ideal age to represent barbaric human value for ransom or labor or worse, Rachel had heard.

Rachel wept for their fates, and for her own, as the living were borne jarringly along among the roiling flight of savages, across the field of the dead.

What transpired afterward at the fort, Rachel did not know until much later.

In the hours and days after the massacre the remaining Parkers enumerated their losses and began to inquire after the hostages. Remaining hidden for some weeks without daring to bury the strewn and disfigured bodies, they sent word as far as President Houston himself, to plead for aid.

Granted none, James Parker—a middle son of the massacred Elder John—soon took it upon himself to leave his surviving household behind and venture out solo in search of the abducted women and children. Some of the clan returned to the fort. Others kept their distance. In his search for the missing, James bore the dangers alone, allowing none of his kinfolk to slow him down or share the considerable risks he vowed to face until he found and returned the captives. As one unsuccessful mission gave way to another, season after season James tracked leads and ran down rumors deep into Indian strongholds.

James W. Parker's obsessive quest became widely known. In his missions he drew deeply on his knowledge of the backwoods and plains and his ability to avoid being killed or captured himself. In solitary he carried on his crusade. Once, nearly freezing to death on the plains north of the Red River when caught out in the open by an October norther, he managed to keep going, following the barest thread of hearsay. A young woman fitting Rachel's description had been spotted among the Kiowas.

Upon the culmination of his arduous journey Parker learned that the unfortunate woman had indeed been a captive, but she was no daughter of his. He had exhausted his horses, exhausted his funds, and exhausted his health and energies, and he trudged home empty-handed.

When the next spring came, Parker took up his quest again, once grazed by an Indian's bullet but outriding the enemy party. In sweltering summer he tracked yet another lead, resorting to leaving his own handwritten messages tied to thorn bushes in regions where Comanche bands were known to camp and hunt.

About James Parker's journeys, the newspapers carried lurid stories in addition to his own advertisements. As far north as the Parker homeland of Illinois, as far east as the meeting houses of legislatures in the United States, as far west as the mountains and as far south as the deserts, word spread of the desperate father scouring the plains for any trace of the missing Rachel, her infant son, and her young cousins. Whites everywhere sympathized, scared they might be the next taken. Those who had extended their residency out to the fringes of the frontier prayed in fervent faith to remain safe; if they felt their God had guided them to this promised land, how could he just abandon them there? No one seemed able to prevent the predations, or predict who would be next.

In private alliance, however, it was rumored that a conclave of influential settlers—primarily German immigrants to the Plains whose women and children continued to suffer similar atrocities at the hands of the savages—began to form a covert plan. Their mission was not known to the public at large, nor likely to their own families, and even decades later was only whispered and speculated about. Money flowed from well outside the borders of Texas, funneled to a close-kept cabal ensconced deep in the new nation.

This undertaking did not make the papers. Like the most clandestine of secret societies across history the network recruited quietly in private chambers, employing a system of cloaked signals, and veiled their activities behind layers of everyday respectability. They swiftly quashed any stirring of rumor, and for that reason their narrative would long remain unknown to those who were otherwise familiar with the very public story of the Parker clan's travails.

They called themselves the Rächer. Their sole aim was fixed, and fiery, and well funded: revenge.

Chapter 9
RACHEL AND HER CHILDREN

{In which Rachel and her progeny are removed far from their kin.}

THROUGH THE LONG DAY AND EVEN LONGER NIGHT the whines and whimpers of Rachel's little boy echoed across the prairie as the babe, ill handled by the jubilant, fleeing captors, sought the solace of its mother. Rachel herself cried out from her own wounds but even more keenly for the injured innocent from whom she had been separated. She knew by now that her uncle, Benjamin, had been killed, as had his father, Elder John, though her grief for them paled in light of her fear. Only her young son's incessant cries led her to know that he still lived.

The People cared nothing for the taibo's agonies; there was an important lesson to be brought home. If the handful of captives they'd suffered to live were worth anything, it was as slaves—or as leverage. The warriors made sure as they dragged the white prisoners away that they'd witnessed the arrow-pierced corpses and speared scalps resulting from the raid. Those who had escaped death this time would pay in a different way.

Buoyed by their victory, and apparently outdistancing any survivors who might have trailed them, the People lashed their prizes to the backs of horses and hauled them like pack goods to a rendezvous point. There they visited more humiliations and mutilations upon this piteous clutch of women and children before determining what to do with them. Ultimately the spoils were divided; best to keep the taibo from talking with their own kind.

Rachel's older cousin Elizabeth, nearly forty and of less immediate interest to the People, was handed off to a band from the K'itaish tribe, who
roamed the eastern part of what was now Texas and beyond and who were
called Kichai or Keechee by the newcomers. That group soon traded her to
Delawares living near the Texas frontier town of Nacogdoches, where scouts
passed along word to the settler communities.

Cynthia Ann, only nine, was sent off with one Comanche band, while
her younger brother, John Richard, was given to another.

Little Robert Pratt Plummer was led off on a journey separate from that
of his mother, Rachel, whose advancing pregnancy with her second child in
time became evident to her captors.

None of the four captives knew the fate of any other, until ransom or
recapture in due time—months, years, decades—brought them back into
their original fold and the public eye.

Inquiries began, loudly in the papers and quietly behind the scenes.
Had matters been left to the wasted armies of Sam Houston, the secretive
German group knew full well, no search party would be mustered. Old Sam
Jacinto himself lay up at Nacogdoches recovering from the wound he'd taken
in that decisive battle, while the dispersed Parkers—still numerous even in
the face of their grievous losses—considered their options. The Parker survivors did not return immediately to their fort on the Navasota. Depleted of
ready resources and without a spring crop, they scattered to the settlements
of other kin at safer removes from the Indians.

The wrathful Rächer, upon learning with disgust that Houston had
declined the Anglo Parkers' entreaty for men and money to go after the
captives, began building their coffers and seeking their moment. When
Houston relented and provided James Parker funds to purchase Elizabeth
Kellogg's freedom from Delaware intermediaries in August 1836, no one
but the highest ranks of the society knew where the $150 in coin came
from. But the secret funders congratulated themselves upon learning more
about Kellogg's kinsman who had made it his singular mission to redeem
and retrieve the captives.

James Parker quietly escorted the ransomed woman back to Texas.
One day, coming upon a straggler Comanche on their horseback journey

homeward from the Red River country where the Delawares had handed
her over, Kellogg whispered to Parker *There, that lance—I would recognize the
gray scalp of our Elder John anywhere.* As further verification she bid him look
for scar marks she still vividly recalled. Finding them, Parker dispatched the
murderous Comanche with the same brutal swiftness the savage had shown
to the patriarch.

"With mingled feelings" of "joy at the opportunity of avenging the butch-
ery of my father, and sorrow at the recollection of it," Kellogg later wrote,
she bore witness. Though her account of her three-month ordeal shocked
readers of Eastern newspapers, it failed to mobilize action from the United
States. In the newly created but destitute Republic of Texas, Houston—who
believed settlement of the frontier to be a long game of forbearance and
diplomacy, and who also sympathized with the natives whose lands the settlers were overtaking—continued to urge patience.

The society of avengers bided its time and watched each new develop-
ment with interest.

It was clear to Rachel Plummer that, rather than traveling closer to what
she considered civilization, their party was pushing farther from it. In those
first days after the capture she could tell only that the riders led them north.
Due to her bruises and the blood that, mingled with sweat, still trickled down
her forehead, she could hardly make out the details of the trek, had she even
known the names for the geography they traversed. From their first camp
north of the Navasota they had entered a billowing sea of gentle grasses
punctuated by streams and small trees. The riding was easy there but the
sun was fierce, and she and the other white-skinned captives suffered severe
sunburn on top of their other pains.

Leaving the prairie they continued northward into a country of thickly
gnarled and stunted oaks and other hardwoods. Rachel had heard tell of
the cross timbers; while the branches of the trees afforded respite from the
unremitting summer sun, the cage of wilderness they formed made for hard
going on horses and left the captives' limbs lacerated as badly as the leather
thongs with which they'd been regularly flogged. Rachel came to covet the
protective tanned-hide garments of the Comanche women.

There was little else about the captors' choices she admired. Meals of
greasy game meat, beds of grass in temporary camps, and daily subjection

to the taunts and abuses of men and women alike: these she endured even as her abdomen swelled and it became clear to all that she would give birth to her next child sometime after the tribe had passed from plains into high mountains, in the fall.

There in what Rachel calculated to be October, in a cove of piñon and cedar where the band's tents were pitched for shelter from autumn snows, her second child came into the world. The newborn, despite her certainty he would emerge weak and small, was healthy enough. His cries and needs annoyed the warriors and their wives. Any hope Rachel might have held for merciful treatment of her brown-haired baby boy was dashed within a few short weeks, as winter arrived in earnest. One day in full view of her, half a dozen grown men seized the infant from her, choked it by the throat and tossed it in the air time after time to land on the frozen, rocky ground. Rachel desperately tried to rescue and resuscitate the injured child, but her tormentors bound its limbs with leather ropes from their horses and, scream-ing savagely, dragged the tiny body repeatedly across outcrops of prickly pear cactus. Sharp spines shredded thin pink skin again and again until no life remained. Rachel pleaded and wept until she could weep no more, then cried out silently to the heavens, promising to find a way, somehow, to dig the innocent soul a decent resting place.

It was a low and cold winter for Rachel, lacking sufficient clothing and lacking any respect from her unconcerned captors. She could muster no enthusiasm for life. The baby murdered in front of her and the older son's fate still a mystery, she imagined that her husband and her father must both have perished in the May massacre like the others. What remained for her, on this earth?

She thought she had no will left in her. But one day in their mountain camp, as the grizzled old Indian woman she served approached her with a club as if to beat her for some offense, Rachel to her own surprise fought back. With no thought to consequences she seized the club and turned on her mistress. As she knocked the old woman to the ground she was certain her mutinous action would immediately bring down the wrath of the entire band. But instead the Indians watched, shouting, and to her even greater surprise praised her. Rachel's spunk had earned a measure of admiration from a warrior people, who from that moment afforded her more humane treatment.

Whatever little hope she may have reclaimed, by spring a miracle came. The Comanches, inexplicably, decided to sell her away.

Chapter 10
THE LONE SEARCHER

{In which a deal is struck.}

"YOU'LL NOT BE ABLE TO CARRY ON YOUR MISSION WITHOUT AID," the stranger said, shrouded in the dark, the hood of a woolen cloak pulled down over his forehead as the early autumn rain drenched the oiled cloth stretched between branches above them. "*Eine Nadel im Heuhaufen,* how goes the old saying, *ja,* a needle in a haystack."

The searcher took another sip of his coffee and edged closer to the small fire he'd risked building. He contemplated the man's words but did not reply.

The man continued, his accent heavy but his English smooth and practiced. "Houston cannot risk bringing another war on himself, this time from the savages. As for the United States, this new president will not let Texas in as long as the republic holds to slavery, and he has big money troubles of his own. You should not expect help there."

The searcher nodded slowly in agreement. Each time he had slogged home to his rude cabin and his frustrated wife, he had renewed his campaign of beseeching letters. The Lord had not, so far, rewarded him. But he would not give up.

"And can you be certain your daughter yet lives, and the young ones?"

"I will not rest as long as there is a chance they do."

The man slipped a plain leather purse from somewhere beneath the brown cloak and handed it across the fire. "I represent a group that has followed your efforts, Mr. Parker. We applaud your determination."

"What group?"

"Avengers."

"Why?"

"Our reasons are much like yours."

"I presume you'll want something in exchange."

The stranger looked up slightly, enough to reveal his eyes in the flickering firelight. They crinkled in a slight smile. "Information, *mein Freund*. Intelligence from the field. You may encounter more captives who are not the ones you seek, and learn of the movements of tribes. For this we pay handsomely."

"How will I share word?"

"One of our number will approach you with a purse like this one. If among the coins you find a single silver *thaler*, invite the man to break bread with you, and then convey to him any details that may be relevant. Commit nothing to paper."

The searcher nodded, absorbing the details. "You know my name but I do not know yours."

The cloaked man pulled the edge of his hood back over his face and stood, crouched beneath the tarpaulin. "Nor will you," he said as he ducked under it and untied the reins of his drenched roan. "*Danke und Gott geh mit dir,* sir. God go with you."

It was on that same venture, pushing northward on foot that fall after he could not swim his horse across the swollen Red River, that James Parker nearly froze to death when an early norther swept across the plains. The captive he'd traveled so far to see turned out not to be his daughter, and he made his weary way home again. From the secret purse he paid informers and other pursuers. He took out a newspaper advertisement offering a reward "For every Prisoner among the Indians that might be Brought In." It had been nearly a year and a half since the attack on his family's fort, and only the thankful Elizabeth Kellogg had come home. On all the vast American continent, among peoples of many tongues and customs, Parker knew nothing more of the captives' whereabouts—or their remains, perish the thought—than he had when he'd started. But he would not rest until he found answers.

One snowy day, high in the Rockies where her baby boy had lived out his brief existence the previous year, a Mexican trader approached Rachel Plummer's Comanche master. Rachel hardly dared believe, hardly dared hope . . . but a negotiation began. Her captor agreed to hear the offer. The men went inside the master's tent while the young captive stood at the open flap and listened. A price was proposed. The wind blew, and Rachel bent to listen more closely. The old woman came and stood nearby too.

Rachel's heart caught in her throat. Who had sent this bargainer? Who had provided the money?

But when the master's answer came, Rachel felt a different swing of the emotional pendulum. He shook his head no. Not enough.

How could that be . . . if a man had come all this way to ransom her, had somehow found her, had come representing her own husband, how could it be not enough? She had no way of knowing who had lived or died, who still cared. Or was she simply being traded as chattel?

Her martyred grandfather would not have given up. Her father would have paid all he had, all he could beg, borrow, steal. Her husband would want her back . . . wouldn't he?

A second figure was named.

Still not enough, said the red man.

The Comanchero trader turned to go.

Rachel's head swam with disbelief.

So close, so close. She must not have been worth it. Not worth a few dollars more, like a lame mare, maimed beyond further use. Like a plow with a broken share, a coat threadbare, a chair beyond repair. Random English words poured back into her brain, gushing, rushing in vowels her voice had not spoken in twenty moons. Vowels? Her bowels felt loose, her gut knotted. Consonants? Words doubled upon themselves like a rushing stream. A dream. No scream would come. She could not stop the flood, like blood, turning her mind to mud. Or snow. She did not know how she would go on. She froze.

She must have dozed, still kneeling in the cold. How long, she could not be certain. Old, used, injured by these infernal Injuns: these were all the feelings she could conjure. Of one thing she was sure. Her body and soul would not endure another season among the savages. She ceased searching for words in her mother tongue. She would simply lie here, hung up in this spot, and never rise.

But after a long while the men's voices resumed. Had she heard right?

Rachel stood stiffly to her leather-clad feet.

The trader offered more.

The master said—had she heard right, again? *Ha-a.* Yes.

The money had been enough.

Rachel was going home to her people.

Part III

{A continuation from the journal of
FRANKLIN C. HOOPER, M.D., A.F.&A.M.}

Chapter 11
A MAN IN CUFFS

{In which Dr. Hooper learns the solution to a long-standing mystery.}

"IT'S A TRAGIC HISTORY and I hope my family may be free of it all these decades later," said the still-handcuffed Jack Plummer to Captain Miles after he'd related at some length the account of his ancestors' massacre. The speaker exhibited a deliberate and formal diction and a quiet voice that made all present lean in to concentrate on his words. "Though as long as Quanah and the Quahadi Comanches walk the earth there are those who continue to seek blood for blood."

"Let us hope you may become free as well," Miles replied. "But while you are still restrained, for the satisfaction of these gentlemen can you explain how the circumstances you've described came to involve yourself?"

Plummer raised the glass of water in his free hand and took a long drink. We'd been confined in the room for some forty minutes and the July sun was now streaming through the open window, making the air close and stifling.

He looked up, straight into Miles's eyes. "How you got this far already is as much a mystery to me as the whole business must be to you," he said. "If there's a vacant place for a chief of the police, sir, I reckon you are the man for it."

"Don't go nominating me for any jobs, please," said Miles wryly. "On the contrary, the broad strokes of this crime, and most of its solution, were clear to me within an hour of arriving on the scene Thursday morning. It is only how your rôle came about that cannot be deduced from the evidence available in the present. The past—despite its lingering clues—remains a region no human may bodily visit."

Plummer turned to the marshal. "If you'll take my word that I won't run," he said, "I shall do my best to bring you up to the present, at least from what I know, since I'm no firsthand witness myself."

"You are saying that you did not personally see Daimmler murdered?" Courtright demanded.

"I did not—but before I explain further, some more recent background is required, if you'll bear with me."

Courtright sighed.

Miles reached over and unlocked the cuffs, and Plummer made to stand up from the edge of the bed, where he was sweating in the direct sunlight.

At this, Courtright drew the pearl-handled pistol from one of his holsters with a swift, flicking motion and trained it on the man. "Sit back down and don't make another move," he ordered.

Though my own experience with the criminal sort was admittedly limited, I gauged Plummer to be hardly the type—his dodging of the law these past two days notwithstanding. But perhaps there'd been something else he'd been dodging as well.

Courtright kept the gun aimed. "Enough lollygagging. Finish up your story, man. Who exactly are you and why have you killed these two?"

The detainee stretched his arms, wincing slightly at the movement, rubbed his wrists in spite of Courtright's warning, then sat ramrod-straight and exhaled slowly before saying more.

"I assure you, I didn't kill either one of them—and I rue the day I crossed paths with the one who's met his doom on the bricks out there. I'll be content enough to be free of his scheme once I tell you the part of the tale known personally to me. Then I shall leave it to you lawmen to figure out what the crimes were and who committed them."

With some hesitation Courtright lowered his pistol and pulled up a chair directly opposite the man, blocking the sun's rays somewhat. "You do the talkin', then, and I'll do the listenin'," he barked at his suspect, then pointed up in my direction. "And I think the doctor here might be a good candidate to do the writin'. Do take pains to get your story straight, Plummer, in case you wind up having to repeat it to a jury."

I did in fact happen to have a notepad in my vest pocket; such prepa-ration was a habit of long standing with me. But I sorely regretted having dashed off without my camera kit. Leaning over the scene like a common newshound, I drew out my pencil and held it at the ready.

"There are those involved who have already paid a far dearer price," Plummer replied cryptically. "For any collusion of which I might be guilty, any punishment I end up suffering would be little in comparison. But I am not a witting conspirator, sirs, and the information I am about to impart to you—as fragmentary as it may be—was disclosed to me only within the past fortnight. You may not immediately grasp how I could allow myself to fall in with such cunning strangers, but I hope you will come to appreciate how desperate I was to redeem my father's legacy and honor his memory. If I am at fault, I believe it is solely in my zeal to right some very old wrongs."

"Go on, then, with the marshal's permission," said Miles. "For I believe I also know some of what you're about to say."

Garrigan returned finally, clattering down the hallway with two lad-der-back chairs, which he hefted as though they were doll's toys and set them on either side of his boss. I, for one, was grateful to sit. I wiped my brow and prepared to take up my ad hoc assignment.

Chapter 12
ONE HOUR WITH RACHEL

{In which the meanings of coded messages are revealed.}

AFTER CLEARING HIS THROAT Jack Plummer spoke calmly, and I can vouch with confidence for the accuracy of his words, as I am able weeks later to refer to my hastily scribbled Pitman shorthand. Although the young man seemed to expend some effort in connecting a jumble of recent events, his relation of the more distant history he'd shared with us was clear and compelling.

He exhaled a long breath and spoke with solemnity, looking from one of us to the other and fixing on each eye.

"There are those who walk this earth just as we do, gentlemen," he began, "but they are not fully human, not with any hope of salvation in this life or the one to come. They were born of the evil seed and shall not be redeemed.

"That, anyway, is the word my grandfather preached. I learned at my father's knee to blame them and learned from my uncle to hate them. The red men were responsible for a multitude of deaths, giving no care to the agony they inflicted in their killings, nor to the anguish of victims' loved ones left behind. And perhaps worse was the torture not of killing but of capturing, for that pain could be renewed each morning and night, and the knowledge that with every new day the ones who had been taken were introduced all over again to fresh assaults against mind and body."

He paused for a second, closed his eyes, and opened them again. "Such terror and suffering were inflicted on my late uncle James Parker's daughter, Rachel. She was my father's first wife."

Garrigan and the others took in this information as though seeing their suspect for the first time.

"I believe you all know of whom I speak. Anyone reading a newspaper for the past four decades is familiar with the story; it has by now become the stuff of legend, though in my extended family the episode is as real to the next generations as it was on the first of May, 1836.

"Rachel Parker Plummer was but one of the many taken or killed among my father's family, not to mention the scores, hundreds, thousands of others tortured and slaughtered by the red savages over the years. She had perpetrated no offense against them. Nor had any of the other innocents. Though Rachel was mercifully ransomed after eighteen months among the savages, and over a long and arduous course turned over to a white family in Santa Fe and eventually returned to Texas, she was never again the same, they said."

Jack Plummer paused again and seemed to summon his thoughts. The small room had grown even warmer with the presence of so many persons, and sweat broke out on his brow. I urged him to continue sipping the water; he drained the rest of the glass before resuming his account. I glanced over at Miles, whose half-lidded gaze betrayed neither shock nor sympathy nor skepticism at anything we had so far heard.

"I never knew Rachel, of course," Plummer continued. "She did not survive long after being ransomed; she died a few days shy of her twentieth birthday, in March of '39. A year then passed before my father, Luther Thomas Martin Plummer, remarried, and another decade before I was born. But I knew some of the others—those whose shame became a matter of public display, or those who told their stories in books. I have read the graphic details from Rachel Plummer's autobiography. Of Cynthia Ann Parker's abduction, long captivity, eventual recapture, and sorrowful passing, you are also surely aware. From my earliest memories I existed with the stigma of these victims, the mental anguish of their kinfolk, and the continual searches and sacrifices of Uncle James Parker, whom many considered deranged. My own father died last year a withdrawn and broken man.

"Thanks to the prurient interests of the press, I imagine some of you know these histories as well as I, though I assure you the details are never quite as depicted.

"Thus, you must also understand that there was never equal punishment done for the red men's crimes. It would have been impossible to single out any of them for trial, though such justice was at times attempted. Now, the savages are far beyond prosecution.

"For many years my Uncle James pursued the captors and murderers, allowing none besides himself to share the risk. He depleted his finances and his health in doing so. I myself, as the recent parent of an infant who perished after a few short weeks on this earth, can hardly fathom the pain of a man who has had a grown daughter so cruelly taken, along with her small child, and his niece and nephew as well. It was said that my father, L.T.M. Plummer, offered no aid in the search. But he paid, as did others, in different ways.

Jack Plummer halted, as though to allow these connections to sink in, then caught his breath and continued. "So there arose among the settler colonies a clandestine plan to address the situation, long before the War between the States left those on the frontier to defend themselves. This is a matter about which I had only the vaguest notion until the events of this week, however, when I was brought into the fold of a certain society. What I am telling you here may well be the first true report to ever reach the ears of authorities, so closely guarded have been this group's activities. I leave it to your judgment what to do with the information, though I plead my innocence of wrongdoing.

"Some of those who hoped to locate and ransom captives and avenge atrocities assembled together covertly. Their confederacy was more secret than societies like the Masons, for not only were their practices veiled in shadow, the organization's very existence was withheld from the public. Certain elements of their conduct would not have met with approval of government or church.

"The founders of this tightly knit alliance were, unlike the Scottish and English Parkers and Plummers, of Teutonic extraction. They quietly represented powerful German business interests in America and sought to back firebrands like some of my forebears, who would do the dirty work of reclaiming captives and exacting retribution. They called themselves the Rächer."

Miles nodded and interjected, "The Avengers. The moneymen who, to defend their investments in their colonies, furnished ransom purses and backed punitive expeditions."

"How do you know about this?" Plummer seemed taken aback, by someone of his own relative youth.

"Let us say . . . service in Mackenzie's most recent expedition yielded useful intelligence," Miles replied. "I am not at liberty to disclose more."

"I was told the Rächer demanded a blood oath for entry," Plummer said, lifting his bandaged arm, "but I didn't mean to give it. As long as that hooligan took such a goodly supply from me, though, I was going to find a way to leave a clue."

Courtright asked, "It was you who wrote the word on the wall here, you're sayin'?" indicating that I should be sure to take down this information.

"Yes, right before you got here. But not at the other place, that—ah, whorehouse—as I read in the paper yesterday."

Courtright pressed his man. "That doesn't make any sense, if, as you say, you didn't join up."

"I'm getting ahead of myself, sir. Allow me to pick up where I left off."

Courtright drummed his fingers on his knee but relented.

"This is all according to that henchman—your dead man—who was out to recruit me. Going back just a few years, you'll recall the alarming incident of young Herman Lehmann, who was taken by the Apaches. The Rächer have funded previous searches for this youth, and the Rangers—who were offered aid, I understand—spotted him among the Indians last year near Fort Concho. But only a couple of months ago word got about that Lehmann had dispatched his Apache captor to the great hunting ground and taken up with the Comanches north and west of Fort Worth."

Plummer, growing hoarse as the sun beat down, asked for his water glass to be refilled. He took a long draught.

"Last week a man showed up as I was plowing in my field, a day's journey from here. I went for the rifle I kept fastened in the mule's harness, as I at first took him for a savage. Savage he was, all right—a half-breed Tonk and a mercenary, I discovered—but he persuaded me to hear him out as I held the gun on him. He introduced himself as Stengel, said he was an agent for several land interests in Texas. He was tall as I and tanned, and he wore a fringed buckskin vest over shirt and trousers. His hair, he wore down to his shoulders, and he was clean-shaven in the Indian manner. He spoke, however, like a white man."

"This Stengel, might he go by the *nom de guerre* of Stinger?" Courtright interrupted.

"I came to learn that, yes. That's the Anglos' nickname for him.'"

Courtright and Miles exchanged a knowing glance.

"Eventually Stinger—Stengel—persuaded me that he needed my family's help, and he considered me—as the eldest surviving son of L.M.T. Plummer and a level-headed man lately settled down with a wife—to be the best candidate to approach.

"He talked of how he worked for men who had helped my Uncle James years ago, and it was just a fair turnabout. That I and my family owed him. He sounded reasonable enough; I invited him to come sit with me in the shade and make his case. I never let my gun get far from my hand, mind you, and neither did he with his.

"His proposal seemed straightforward. He said that in recent weeks, the Rächer had learned the whereabouts of the Texan, Herman Lehmann, who had been taken by the Comanches. This boy had been turned completely to the ways of the Comanche, to the extent that he fought alongside them as they attacked settlements of his own people. So deeply had this youth been manipulated, said Stinger, that he might not come willingly if rescue were attempted. The key to a successful exchange with traders would be an emissary who could reason with the boy, someone who sympathized with a captive's experience. None of my returned Parker or Plummer kin still lived; that episode had been forty years ago. My own father had shown no inclination to affiliate with the cause of the Rächer that I know of, but after his death I suppose I was simply next in line—and easily persuaded to lend aid.

"I promised to give the matter thought, and I expected first to discuss the matter with my wife. I reasoned with myself that, being of tender age and generous disposition, she would have understood that I must do my part in the redemption of a young Christian from the savages. But Stinger said I was to tell no one. After bidding him good-bye, then, I pledged to myself to accept the mission—reluctantly without my wife's knowledge or blessing. I left a note that I had been called away on a pressing errand, and I arranged quietly for a neighbor to see to my fields during what was to be a week's absence.

"I waited the following day for Stinger, and when he appeared at the boundary of my field as before, I shouldered my pack and followed him. We walked the few short miles from Springfield to the train station, where we boarded for the trip north to Dallas and on to Sherman, almost as far as the

Red River. My wife and other kin, it occurred to me once we were aboard, knew not where I was headed, nor had they laid eyes on the man I traveled with. I was instructed to send no message of my whereabouts; secrecy, said Stinger, was of utmost importance to the success of the mission. This should have given me pause, but my companion and I remained within the scope of civilized cities and within the safety of fellow travelers."

Miles broke in. "At your stopover in Dallas, did your companion perhaps take the opportunity to send a telegram?"

"How did you know?" Plummer asked, his brows knitting together as though he had begun to suspect some trap.

"It was Stinger's prearranged signal, to alert others where he planned to deliver a captive," Miles explained.

"I did not know the substance of the message."

"'Engine is in FW.' It was his code—as in red Injun—to let Councilman Daimmler know he should have the ransom money ready. The message, dated 19 July, was found in Daimmler's pocket."

At this, Courtright snorted. "What hogwash! We already have it on good authority that the telegram meant the train, where John Smith would make the drop for Daimmler."

"I was on that very train, Marshal, as the doctor here can attest," said Miles. "There were no other civilian passengers. But I have encountered the code in other situations. I suspected it at once in this case."

I took in this exchange with a keen sense of satisfaction that might have verged on pride. With surgical skill the young captain began to excise the marshal's faulty theory from the vein of truth.

"I'll venture a guess here that Daimmler had been led to expect the triumph of redeeming the famous Lehmann from his captors, with the aid of Stinger," said Miles. "But Lehmann had evaded the deal on its very eve, and Stinger found himself empty-handed—the money gone, and also the boy. To soften the blow and aid in renewed efforts, he recruited Plummer. How impressed Daimmler would be, Stinger reasoned, with a member of the next Parker generation brought into the fold!"

Jack Plummer nodded his assent. "It was exactly as you say, but I learned this only after I was already enmeshed in his plans. Believe me, I would never have been attracted into their web had I suspected the insidiousness of their methods."

"Perhaps you'll describe more fully the events of Wednesday evening, then," suggested Miles. Courtright shifted his weight and crossed his arms.

Plummer plunged in. "Sometime after eleven, when darkness had overtaken the quarter and activity on the street had yielded to its nighttime rhythms, Stinger suggested we should venture out. It was only a few blocks' walk from the hotel here, but he wore a dark slicker and hood and carried an umbrella. The evening was warm; I had only a broadcloth jacket and no hat. We turned the corner onto a particular block which was almost devoid of foot traffic; my companion explained that the working girls who resided there were on duty at the parlors. We stopped in front of a crib with its front windows boarded up. Stinger said it would provide a quiet spot to rendezvous.

"I was to wait silently in the dark side alley, as Stinger laid out the plan, and I was to enter the house when signaled for. I took up my place in the alleyway as told. It began to rain lightly, and I ducked under the shelter of the eave, a station that also afforded me a listening post beneath one of the windows.

"In a few minutes—possibly ten or so—I detected a careful opening and closing of the front door followed by footfalls down the corridor. Hoping to listen more readily I picked my way farther down the alley in tandem with the footsteps; these could not have belonged to Stinger, who was shod in moccasins. They must have been those of the associate Stinger was expecting.

"From beneath the half-open window I could make out the tone of the pair's conversation, though not always its particulars. I could not, however, see in, as the ground inclined downward, so the windowsills of the room where they halted were a foot or so above my head."

Courtright interrupted with a pointed question. "Mr. Plummer, I'd be interested to know how you consider yourself to be an eyewitness if, as you admit, you were not in a position to see at all?"

"Indulge me a bit longer, and I'll get to that," Plummer replied. "I could not see at floor level how the room was furnished. But I had a view of the upper part of the wall, where the wallpaper was torn and stained. A candle had been placed on a mantel, the top of which was visible to me. My curiosity regarding what was being said was just about to get the best of me, especially as I was led to think I myself would be the subject of discussion, but I held to my situation and strained to hear.

"Stinger, whose voice I recognized, spoke first. His words seemed curious. 'I have brought with me the pipe of peace as a sign of my sincere intent,' he said. 'Let us begin with a smoke, which opens our vision into the minds of our enemies and shows us the path to victory,' or something like that. His visitor was amenable.

"I heard the sound of a pouch being shaken, and then that of a match struck against a floorboard. All was silent, but immediately the aroma of burning leaf wafted down through the window toward me. It was not any like that of any tobacco I recognized. Its smoke was more exotic and weedy, sharp on the nostrils.

"After a few moments I heard the other man ask, 'So, Stengel, we are celebrating the return of the'—I don't know the word in German, but I think he meant 'captive.' You have brought him to the city tonight?'"

"The man whose true name I had just overheard answered only that he had a visitor he wanted him to meet. I began to get a bad feeling about this arrangement . . . if my host had not been honest with his associate, was I certain he had been straight up with me? The man said something about the account of Lehmann's return already being drafted for the newspapers—it would be a marvelous triumph, *wunderbar.*"

"At times their talk became intense but it also dipped too low for me to make out the words. What I could readily discern, though, was a growing sentiment of disagreement as Stinger admitted he had *not* brought the boy but rather a man he hoped to introduce into the fold. This plan did not seem to go over well with his associate. Then I heard my own name, the mention of which caused me alarm rather than pride.

"'Plummer is waiting right outside for my signal,' he said.

"As the men's argument turned from simmer to boil I began to wonder if I should make my escape, or how. All of my possessions besides my purse were back in the hotel room, which was not registered in my name and for which I had no key. I was completely unarmed. I had no way of leaving the scene except by foot, a plan that I worried might be easily trackable in that quarter given the bit of rain we'd had. I did not know the lay of the land except in the most general terms. It had become a dangerous predicament, and I rued that I had allowed myself to be dragged into it.

"An idea slowly formed, however, as I considered how I might give Stengel the slip. Knowing he would be able to trace my steps, I determined to deliberately walk in a direction that would indicate I had chosen to return to the hotel . . . then remove my shoes and take a different tack. I might find a suitable place to lie low until an opportunity arose to retrieve my belongings and leave this infernal city.

"I judged it to have been after midnight before I screwed up the courage to act. By this time an even more curious exchange was going on in the room above me. The German was complaining of apoplexy brought on by their altercation. Stengel offered a remedy. 'Take this, Herr Daimmler,' he said, and in that instant I learned the other man's name. But in another instant, just as I was turning to leave my scant shelter, I heard a thud as though a weight had dropped to the floor. The windows in the rickety building rattled. I knew my time had come. I made myself take measured steps back up the slope and onto the sidewalk as though I had left completely at my leisure. I walked the rest of the block exposed in the lamplight, willing myself not to look over my shoulder, then quickly turned onto the main street. There, a bit of wee-hours activity was still going on.

"I made the instant decision to enter an establishment of the kind where I had never before set foot: I removed my boots, took them in my hand, and walked unshod up the steps and into the cozy foyer of the first bordello I encountered.

"I explained to the hostess that I was not seeking companionship but rather the opposite, and asked if she might accommodate me for a place to sleep off an evening's bacchanal. I proffered a fee I hoped might be persuasive. But she said the rooms were already full—she winked, in fact, when she teased that some were already triple occupancy—"

At this, Garrigan, who'd been yawning, couldn't suppress a hoot of laughter. "That's rich! Greenhorn holes up in a whorehouse!"

"Give it a rest, Garrigan," Courtright ordered. "Wouldn't be the first time that strategy's worked. Go on, Mr. Plummer."

"I begged her to at least let me exit out the back. 'Don't know who's on your tail,' she said, 'but I'm not looking for trouble here.' She escorted me to the courtyard at the rear of the building, where I found a gate leading to the alley. I sat down on a crate for a spell, put my boots back on, and pondered my next move.

"Ultimately I made my way back toward the crib where I'd left the two men, hoping to confirm they had departed. Arriving at the place from the alley, I glanced upward to see the light from the side window, just as before. I could not determine whether my host was there, or departed. It was almost dawn, and I ventured out onto the sidewalk, where nothing stirred except a lone hackney cab and the solitary figure of the lamplighter about to douse the lights. Farther up the street a beat cop—maybe one of you gents, I wonder?—was making his way along, glancing down the side alleys.

"Suddenly I saw out of the corner of my eye a flicker of the candle and the shadow of a man silhouetted against the wall. Stengel was still there! I moved fast, reaching into my pocket for the bills I had offered the madam, and approached the lamplighter. Would he allow me to take his place for a moment? Hell, he said, for that wad I could have the whole kit. I donned his hat and scarf, snatched his ladder, and dashed to the next lamppost, where I climbed up and made as though to tend to the lamp. I turned down the wick just before the figure of Stengel strode out of the crib, holding a bloodied handkerchief to his face. He walked beneath me, head down, no doubt tracking my footsteps from a few hours earlier. A block farther on, he stopped, looked around, and hailed the cab, which took him in the direction of the hotel.

"I stood on the ladder long enough to confirm he was out of sight before I climbed down and carried the ladder with me to the window where I'd stood in the pitch dark. I set the ladder up against the clapboards and made my way quietly up to where I could see inside.

"And what a shock I had! I almost fell down at the sight. Smeared on the wall in big, messy letters, in what looked like red paint, was a message."

Courtright held up his hand to signal silence from all. "And what was that message, Mr. Plummer?"

"A German word. The one I'd heard Stengel use. *Räche*—revenge."

"Did you see anything else?"

"I climbed up two more steps to peek over the sill. About that time the candle flickered and went out. But not before I made out the body of a man all contorted on the floor, surrounded by blood. Looked like the person Stengel had brought me to meet was out cold."

As Miles and the lawmen absorbed these last of Plummer's words, the room went quiet except for the soft scratchings of my pencil, which was now quite in need of sharpening. Even the blasé and impatient Courtright seemed caught up in the man's story.

"All well and good, man, though it's only your testimony we have on it, and hardly an ironclad story at that," Marshal Courtright said at last. "And meanwhile, we've got one dead body taking up space in this hotel's ice room and another one uptown in the morgue—and a city council expecting some answers."

Miles prompted the witness for the next part of the story. "And what did you do next with that information, Mr. Plummer? Did you go to the authorities?"

Plummer hung his head. "Sorry to say, I didn't. I was in urgent need of sleep and some way to clear my head—then get out of this deplorable city. I made my way toward the hotel, finishing up the lamplighter's job along the way, and when I reached it, I left the ladder in the courtyard. I had to rest before I could even figure out what to do. But Stinger—whom I now suspected to be a murderer—was in the room with my belongings, you see! I found a park bench for a nap where I could keep an eye out, But my eyes wouldn't stay open. I could not tell you when or if the man left. I knew nothing to do by nightfall except carry out the lamplighter's evening rounds from unlit lamp to lamp, and nothing the next dawn except to conduct the morning ones. I could tell the police were onto the crime by then, and I had picked up a paper and read the gruesome news about the man whose name I had heard.

"I hastened back to the hotel again with the ladder, and this time, as I was stowing it in the courtyard at daybreak, I glanced around the wall and saw a figure that cast terror in my heart. Stinger himself was striding down the walkway. But to my relief he passed on without so much as looking in my direction and entered the café across the way. I saw my chance. The window of the room above, which I gauged to be the one we had occupied, had been left open. I steeled my courage, proped the ladder against the second-story sill, and climbed up and inside.

"I had almost finished gathering my possessions, as I intended to exit the way I'd come, when I heard a key being inserted into the lock and saw the handle of the door turn. I contemplated diving underneath one of the beds but had no time. Within another second I was standing face to face with the man who knew I was about to absquatulate."

"Ab—*what?*" asked the marshal.

"Cut and run," I interjected, not looking up from my notebook until I realized I had spoken aloud. Plummer, impassioned in the telling of his story, hardly missed a beat.

"Stinger pulled a knife as fast as a magician," he said, gesturing with his good arm and pointing in the direction of the recent action. "I tried to evade him, but there was no path of escape except the way I'd come. I backed toward the open window and before I knew it he came at me with the blade; it was some sort of miracle that he tripped on the carpet just as he would have grabbed my collar. In a flash he went sailing through the window, pushing the ladder out in front of him as he went. He managed to slash through my sleeve on his way down.

"I closed my eyes in that moment but can only imagine him tangled in the ladder and unable to stop a fall onto the bricks. I then looked out the window as he uttered only a short gasp and lay there, immoble. Whether he was dead or merely injured, I could not tell, and I could not yet risk an exit. I also had no money left, and now was responsible for the damaged ladder, with no easy way to earn more. I pondered a plan for too long . . . once I saw the lawmen arrive and you two head for the entrance"—he indicated me and Miles—"I looked for a hiding spot. I fear I have not acted nobly."

Marshal Courtright let this flood of information sink in, mulling it for a full five seconds. "Mr. Plummer, I think you'll need to repeat your account for the magistrate," he said. "But there is one point on which I'd like a little more information. What about the parlor token in the victim's pocket? How does that figure into all this?"

Plummer shook his head. "I've no clue."

Miles stood. "I can shed some light here, Marshal. While this metal disc may look like one that's issued by the brothels, in this case it's a challenge of identity. As a silver dollar might've been used before the war. A member of the Rächer would show it as a discreet sign; if the gesture produced a matching token, discussions could proceed, details could be shared."

Courtright nodded in consideration, then dispatched Garrigan and Crow to transport the second body uptown.

"You, Mr. Plummer, come with me," he said to the exhausted suspect. "We've got a judge to see." I noted that at least no one had moved to pull out the cuffs again.

Chapter 13
THE CRIMSON THREAD

{In which the hatred of generations is considered.}

ON THE FOLLOWING TUESDAY EVENING as I entered our digs bearing a sack with beef-liver sandwiches for supper and a newspaper from the corner hawker, Derrick Miles was seated in the armchair and already hidden behind an open copy of the *Democrat*.

He peered over the top of the sheet at me, his dark eyebrows cocked in different directions in an expression of wry consternation.

"You've made it well past the headline already, I see," I responded.

He slammed the paper closed and proceeded to wad it into a ball and toss it onto the hearth, where the coals stood cold and impotent in late July's sweltering heat.

I set the sack down on the table and read aloud from my own copy. "Itinerant Indian Fingered in Daimmler Demise," I said. "Seems accurate, no?"

"Read on," Miles prompted.

A smaller subhead stated, "Murderer Killed in Fall While Eluding Lawmen." I pondered the editor's choice of words. "Also to the point." I wasn't sure where he was going with this.

"Here, hand me the story and I'll skip to the heart of it," he said.

"As long as you won't waste my dime too," I answered, pointing to the copy he'd discarded in his pique. "I haven't had the chance to peruse the classifieds. I may yet require calmer lodgings if only for my health and sanity."

Ignoring this, Miles scanned down the columns of type, folding the sheet just so before reading a portion of the text to me as I settled into the chair opposite him. "The public," he intoned, "have lost the opportunity to see in the dock the man who has emerged as the presumptive killer of Mr. Ernst Daimmler, councilman of Fort Worth, a week ago in the city. The full details of the case will probably be never known now, though we are informed upon good authority that the crime was the result of an old standing association, in which revenge and ransom bore a part. This information emerged as part of a magistrate's hearing in city court this morning, during which rampant speculations of the past week appear to have been settled following a week of forensic investigation.

"POISON THE CAUSE. Mr. Daimmler was dispatched to his death around midnight last Wednesday night or early Thursday morning at a Rusk Street address by administration of a potent poison, according to careful detective work by the city marshal's office under the leadership of recently elected marshal Timothy I. Courtright. According to the marshal, whose associates had assiduously gathered and analyzed numerous aspects of evidence from the crime scene, Daimmler had arranged a meeting with one Stengel, an occasional scout and informant and an Indian half-breed, at the unoccupied Rusk Street house for an unknown purpose. There the councilman was crossed by his informant and duped into ingesting a dose of strychnine.

"WRITTEN IN BLOOD. It was previously made known to the public in these pages that, before departing the house, Stengel used the victim's own blood to write upon the wall the word 'Rache,' German for 'revenge'. Further testimony in today's proceedings, combined with evidence from an autopsy, suggested that the blood instead belonged to Stengel himself, who had suffered a broken nose in an altercation with Daimmler on the fateful evening.

"A DOUBLE DEATH. Although police traced Stengel's whereabouts within hours Thursday morning to a hotel near the stockyards, Marshal Courtright and his deputies arrived just in time to discover that the suspect had flung himself from the window of his second-storey room and had expired upon the brick paving of the courtyard, where the man's body was soon reported by a distressed passer-by. Another possible witness at the hotel was detained for questioning by the judge in chambers but was released on his recognizance. Neither of these names was released to the newspaper.

"MAGISTRATE REMANDS SMITH CASE TO MARSHALS. In light of evidence regarding the true cause of Councilman Daimmler's death, clerk John Smith, who was arrested Thursday and held in the city jail upon suspicion of murder and extortion, was today cleared of the murder charge but turned over to custody of the U.S. Marshal's office pending trial for charges of extortion.

"The citizens of Fort Worth are no doubt taking pride in the persistence and shrewdness of the city's new marshal and his able-bodied aides, deputies Arthur Crow and Gormlaith Garrigan. These men owe a portion of debt to the unconventional research techniques of Capt. Derrick Miles, late of Fort Griffin and recently arrived in the city, whose amateur experiments into qualities of toxins and human blood proved useful in gathering evidence.

"Courtright and his two officers are scheduled to be presented with commendations at tomorrow's city council meeting. Announcement of an appointment to fill Daimmler's unexpired term on council is also on the agenda."

With that Miles slapped the paper on his knee, but I snatched it from him before he could take out more of his ire on my copy.

"I don't see that Courtright and crew really had much to do with solving the case," I said, with what I hoped would strike a sympathetic tone. Even after a week's acquaintance, my companion's temperament and manner of thinking and acting perplexed me.

"What you *do* in this world is a matter of no consequence," he replied bitterly. "The question is, what can you make people *believe* that you have done."

"Such a cynical view, in one so young," said I.

"'Other dogs bite their enemies,'" he replied cryptically. "'I bite my friends to save them.' Cynicism's suffered a bad reputation over the centuries since Diogenes, I contend. I hold only to the ancients' rigorous exercise of reason, a power most people seem to have forgotten they possess. Take this case, for instance: it was a simple one, really, and any of these lawmen *could* have traced the same chain of events backwards from the evidence and identified the murderer within three days, just as I myself did."

"Simple? I'm the one not following you."

"Most people, if you describe a train of events to them, will tell you what the result would be. They can put those events together in their minds, and argue from them that something will come to pass. There are few people, however, who, if you told them a result, would be able to evolve from their own inner consciousness what the steps were which led up to that result. This power is what I mean when I talk of reasoning backwards, or analytically."

As Miles appeared to have abandoned his irritability and settled in to wax philosophical, I took the opportunity to sit and open up the sandwiches before us. I poured us each a whisky and let him expound at will.

"Let's start, in the case at hand, with what information was available to us last Wednesday night. Approaching the house on foot from the corner, and with my mind a blank slate free of prejudice, I naturally began by examining the roadway, and there, as I have already explained to you, I saw clearly the marks of a cab, which, I ascertained by inquiry, must have been there during the night. I satisfied myself that it was a cab and not a wagon by the narrow gauge of the wheels, and not a buggy or trap by the length of its wheelbase.

"This was the first point ascertained. I then walked slowly down the alley, which happened to be composed of a red clay soil, peculiarly suitable for taking impressions. Courtright and his force—and you yourself—might've seen only a trampled course of weeds and damp dust, but to my trained eyes every mark upon its surface had a meaning. There is no branch of detective science which is so important and so much neglected as the art of tracing footsteps. From my youngest days I had been coached in the ways of tracking man and beast in the wilderness, but during my studies in London I came to appreciate the techniques of reading human pathways in busy cityscapes. I saw the heavy footmarks of the deputies, but I saw also the track of the two men who had first passed that way. It was easy to tell that they had been before the others, because in places their marks had been entirely obliterated by the others coming upon the top of them. In this way my second link was formed, which told me that the nocturnal visitors were two in number: one tall (as I calculated from the length of his stride) and shod in soft-soled footwear, and the other heavy-set and fashionably dressed, to judge from the small and elegant impression left by his boots. In the event, it turned out that the involvement of a third man had been deliberately and successfully obscured, as Plummer later told us he had walked in his stocking feet to erase his earlier prints and leave none to be traced.

"On entering the house I found confirmation of the two participants. My well-booted man lay prone for all to see. The tall one, then, had done the murder, if murder there was. There was no wound upon the dead man's person, so the copious blood was not his—but the tortured expression upon his face assured me that he had been stirred by extreme anger before meeting his fate. Men who die from heart disease, or any sudden natural cause, never by any chance exhibit agitation upon their features. On the dead man's lips as I bent to sniff, I detected a slightly sour smell, and I concluded that poison had been given to him, or forced on him. I leaned toward the theory it had been proffered, as the two figures had spent some time in animated, even heated, discussion and forcible poisoning did not seem as likely. In the *raiz diabólica*—peyote—that might have been used in a ceremony such as Plummer described overhearing—are alkaloids related to those in strychnine. By the method of exclusion, I had arrived at this result, for no other hypothesis would meet the facts. The surreptitious administration of poison is by no means a new thing in criminal annals, as you may know; here, the extreme contortions of the face and body and the swift death were giveaways to strychnine. The instance of McCauley of Glasgow, who ingested rat poison brought over on his ship from India after mistaking it for quinine powder, as well as the case of the unfortunate Delachaise in New Orleans, will occur at once to any toxicologist who keeps up with the journals."

"I'm afraid I haven't had call to, myself," I interjected, as though his declamation had been a personal challenge. "Poison wasn't a common cause of death in field hospitals."

Miles gave a sideways nod of acknowledgment but continued his discourse, a rushing river impeded only briefly by a log swept swiftly downstream. "In time, Stengel's possession of another dose, in an unmarked bottle, further confirmed to me that he was in the habit of employing this method of killing. He may even have intended the last pill for Plummer after learning of his would-be accomplice's refusal."

I silently considered the unpleasant possibility that we might have had another death on our hands, had Miles not set his Panther Cubs to work so quickly.

"But back to the initial case," said Miles. "Now came the great question as to motive. Robbery had not been the object of the murder, for nothing was taken despite easy access to numerous items of value. Was it a woman, then, or money, or politics? That was the question which confronted me. I was inclined from the first to the former supposition. Political assassins operate in secret and flee. Money had been ruled out. This killing had, on the contrary, been prepared for in case it was needed, and the perpetrator had left his tracks all over the room, showing that he had been there all the time. The parties knew each other well. It must have been a private wrong, and not a political one, which called for such methodical steps. When the inscription was discovered upon the wall I was more inclined than ever to my opinion. Someone was pointing a finger—and not at a woman, though this is how he designed the message to be read.

"A cunning figure, I reasoned, accustomed to covering his tracks. I then proceeded to make a careful examination of the room, which confirmed my opinion as to the murderer's height, and furnished me with the additional details as to length of his nails and hair. I had already come to the conclusion, since there were no signs of a struggle, that the blood which covered the floor had burst from the murderer's own nose in his excitement or struggle. I could perceive that the traces of blood coincided with the track of his feet. It is seldom that any man, unless he is very full-blooded, breaks out in this way through emotion, so I hazarded the opinion that the perpetrator was probably a robust and ruddy-faced man—and that the victim had gotten off a lucky punch to his enemy's lip or nose before expiring. Events proved that I had judged correctly.

"The term our killer chose to write appeared calculated to misdirect the police—but also to send a coded warning to insiders. When the token was found, however, it settled the question. It was a perverse choice of signal, and therefore calculated to mislead officers of the law. Ophelia Dixon's information ruled out any supposition on that front. Then, even lacking special knowledge of the German group and their occult methods, as I possessed, one would have next turned to identifying and locating the tall stranger. You recall how I established the circumstances of this person's arrival with an umbrella."

I nodded yes.

"Even so, I originally drew a mistaken line between Moccasins and the lamplighter," he said. I was surprised to hear him admit as much. "We may be thankful that Deputy Garrigan's chance mention provided a necessary clue."

"But back to umbrella-man. If he had come to keep an appointment," Miles said, pausing to underscore the plain logic of his deduction by templing his fingers together, "then it stood to reason he must be lodged somewhere in the city. I therefore organized my street arab detective corps, and took the obvious step of polling every hotel in Fort Worth until they ferreted out the man I wanted. The Panther Cubs succeeded only a few moments too late.

"The death of Stengel was an incident which was entirely unexpected, but which could hardly in any case have been prevented. Through it, as you know, we came into possession of the powder, the existence of which I had already surmised, and was able to show this link to the police. You see the whole thing is a chain of logical sequences without a break or flaw."

Apparently the stream of discourse had leveled out and reached its delta. Miles drained the last of his whisky glass and stood to gaze out the window at the rising moon.

I raised my own glass in pronounced congratulation. "This is nothing short of amazing!" I cried. Already my diffidence, even outright suspicion, had waned regarding my accidental housemate's character. I found myself taking his side. "The public's misperceptions must be set to rights. You should write an account of this case for the journals. Or *I* will—I have notes to go by. Your story needs to be told!"

"Do as you wish, Doctor," Miles replied. "I don't see much profit in it. The marshal and his buffoons are going to get the credit one way or another, and the result of all our sound and fury and careful detection will be to get the bunch a slap on the back and a raise! But at least we can take heart in two beneficial outcomes. First, Jack Plummer is headed home to his wife, with this distasteful chapter in his domestic tranquility closed before it had even had a chance to sink in fully."

"And the second?"

"The end may have come for the clandestine Rächer, absent their two most potent forces," replied Miles, clasping his hands beside his back. "We may never identify every one of those shadowy figures who financed the operation, but we may look for their network to diminish, and hope for the cycle of ransom and retaliation to wind down. Stengel's scheme to pin his crime on a scapegoat was foiled by the crimson thread itself. And as for young Lehmann's whereabouts . . . we may yet gain some information from other useful sources."

I gave this last statement some thought. *What had I gotten myself into?*, I asked mentally for the second time in a week. I refreshed both our glasses and risked another inquiry.

"Regarding those sources, Captain, might they bear any connection to the 'long story' you delayed in telling when we chanced upon Ranger McDonald last week?"

"All in good time, Hooper, all in good time." As Miles settled back into the comfort of his established chair and sipped his Jameson's, he pointed to the *Democrat* copy he'd handed back to me. "You may also note in the pages of your newspaper there that our local 'study in crimson' has been largely overshadowed by a revenge drama still playing out on a national stage."

"Events in the Dakota territory, you mean?"

"Custer's tragedy may be the end of an act but hardly the end of the play. More will come of it, for the Indians and for the army, and my own testimony may soon be needed in the nation's capital," he replied.

Before I could ponder this in more detail, Miles adroitly pivoted. "What do you say, Doctor Hooper, to a journey east for both of us? A summer's excursion might be just the ticket . . . now that it's such an easy matter to catch a train from the Panther City to just about anywhere? The Centennial Exposition is under way in Philadelphia, as you've no doubt been reading."

"Well, I had seen that the National Photographic Association is to meet there on the fifteenth of August as part of the festivities—"

"Say, especially, if such a journey might include attendance at the forthcoming lecture to the Medical Congress by Britain's Doctor Joseph Lister—you may have heard of him—on the antiseptic properties of carbolic acid? Unless the unlikely instance should arise that I am mistaken, I predict Doctor Lister's techniques, which I observed briefly while at university in London, will do no less than revolutionize the practice of surgery and greatly reduce mortality worldwide. I think you might find it quite . . . illuminating."

"I suppose so . . . " My mind spun with anticipation of such an unimagined future.

"I've taken the liberty of telegraphing ahead to arrange for tickets. Miss Whissell was once again most helpful. I've secured an invitation for you."

"Why, I, I—"

"Tongue-tied, Hooper?" Derrick Miles asked in amusement, as he leaned and retrieved two items from the side table: his violin case; and a block of writing paper. The musical instrument he set in his lap; the paper he handed to me. About the size and thickness of a quarto magazine, the pad of lined stock was backed with gray pasteboard, fronted with red paper cover, and bound at the top edge with a sort of gum.

"Picked this up at a stationer's in St. Louis during my recent travels. A fellow was thinking of taking the product to market. I said I could readily see its utility in the field."

"The drawing on the front—yours?" I asked. The figure in full feathered headdress was rendered in profile. The red chief's stern, aquiline nose reminded me of the real-life one at which I was staring.

"Yes, but you're welcome to it," Miles said nonchalantly. "Sounds like you might have a bit of composition to do."

THE END

ACKNOWLEDGMENTS

To write under the guise of a different name presents unique challenges for an author, as I learned in promoting the first book in this series. *The Wolf Hunt: A Tale of the Texas Badlands* sought to transport the familiar and often-imitated fictional characters of Victorian England's detective Sherlock Holmes and his chronicler Doctor John Watson to the American West of their same era.

A male pseudonym sounded like the right marketing strategy. Not only did it seem the height of cheek for a woman to jump into the business of Sherlockian pastiche—time-honored as the practice had come to be—but there was good reason to forestall confusion with my academic works or other novels. I imagined, too, that the publisher generous enough to accept the manuscript—Five Star/Gale Cengage—would succeed better in its standing-order library sales by introducing new author Will Brandon to its Western list.

I underestimated what to do, however, when it came time to take the book on signings or blog tours. How awkward would it be for me to read the part of Watson's analogue, Doctor Frank Hooper? How arrogant still to represent the venerated voice of detective Holmes as Derrick Miles, captain, U.S. Army? I'd painted myself into a corner.

In the event, it didn't matter much. Covid-19 delayed October 2020 publication of *The Wolf Hunt* and did away with in-person events throughout that year. By the time the book came out in 2021, traditional marketing activities remained uncertain. Aside from the offbeat stunt of publishing the first four chapters in serial form in *The Texas Spur* newspaper (a nod to those olden days of Dickens and Doyle), I did little to help the book along.

In the depths of the pandemic I turned my attentions instead to the next tale in the series. If *The Wolf Hunt* reimagined my favorite Holmes thriller—*The Hound of the Baskervilles*—in Fort Worth and remote Dickens

County, Texas, in October 1891, what was the characters' backstory? How did Miles and Hooper meet to start with, and how did they get there?

The event in the true history of West Texas that best represented this origin myth, to my mind, was the arrival of the Texas & Pacific Railway in Fort Worth on July 19, 1876. It was the Promontory Point moment for the Lone Star State, connecting the Union Pacific's vigorous activity to the west and north with the eastbound push to reboot Texas settlement after the devastations of the Civil War. It was also a moment that galvanized the claims of white settlers and the U.S. army over the last stronghold of the Comanches, who had been pushed onto reservations a few months earlier. Set against the national shock of Custer's recent rout at Little Big Horn by the Sioux and their allies, the story must somehow involve the long conflict between indigenous peoples and colonizing aggressors.

Thus this book came to answer Arthur Conan Doyle's own book that famously depicted westward migration on the American continent: *A Study in Scarlet*, whose unsympathetic portrayal of the Mormons brought down indignant criticism on its author and an eventual apology from him.

A Study in Crimson, like its model, frames the story of an Anglo, male detective partnership around that of an "other" antagonist. It's my hope that this fictional work presents a subplot respectful to the Comanches and other native groups, as well as to marginalized religious fundamentalists. Historian Susan C. Miller contends that it's not possible for non-natives to write responsibly about Indian lifeways or thought, and wrongheaded for them to try. I'd like to believe that's not entirely so, and that the medium of fiction can deliver truth among a mix of historical fact

Fort Worth Democrat, July 20, 1876

and outright invention.

And while we're talking about assuming the identity of another, let me also express my hope that critics will forgive (maybe even appreciate?) in this series the lifting of isolated passages from the originals. I challenge readers to spot and celebrate such phrases—by my count, a dozen instances of varying lengths in this book—that should stand as recognizable landmarks on a journey through newly replowed territory.

If we seek to blur the lines that define and segregate our shared society, this white female writer would say, a bit of appropriation is worthwhile in the process.

Writers of factual history have provided essential background to the series of Derrick Miles novels. In this one, I particularly appreciated the well-documented blog "Hometown by Handlebar," by bicyclist and former *Fort Worth Star-Telegram* columnist and travel writer Mike Nichols (mikenichols. org), which helped form a reliable snapshot of the Panther City circa 1876. I regret never having corresponded with Nichols; I learned of his passing in 2022, just as I was wrapping up this draft to offer it for reading.

Biographies of "Longhair Jim" Courtright, Texas Ranger Captain William J. "Bill" McDonald, and the celebrated madams of Hell's Half Acre provided verifiable details.

The aerial-view map "Fort Worth, Tarrant County, Texas," drawn in April 1876 by D. D. Morse, held by the Amon Carter Museum, and made available for reference on Wikimedia Commons, perfectly lays out the geography of this story. (Later counterparts inform the 1891 opening scene of the first book in this series.)

Among the many accounts of the Parker family massacre and its aftermath, from contemporary screeds to first-person memoirs to scholarly treatises, I turned to two I trusted would undergird this imagined version with thorough documentation: Jo Ella Powell Exley, *Frontier Blood: The Saga of the Parker Family* (Texas A&M University Press, 2001), and Marybeth Weston, *The Comanche with the Blue Eyes: The Story of Frontier Captive Cynthia Ann Parker,* the stage play with expanded essays and notes. (Hanaba Munn Welch, who contributed so much to that work, also lent her copious historical knowledge and excellent word sense to this one.) These resources cite many valuable primary texts, such as Rachel Plummer's own captivity narrative, which I also read and absorbed.

Information about German-American captive Herman Lehmann used in this story also hews as closely as possible to verified fact—though the tale of the fictional Rächer is a complete fabrication. If any such group of avengers ever existed, it is as unknown to history as it was to the character, here, of John Wesley "Jack" Plummer—a historical personage borrowed for the tale as was his grandmother Rachel.

Rachel Parker Plummer, 1819–1839 (Geni.com)

The circumstances and customs of the Texas frontier are, likewise, harvested from recorded history. From the 1876 arrival of the Texas & Pacific Railway, to the conveyances, camera equipment, clothing, cops, communications, and cures of the era, to the groundbreaking lecture of England's Doctor Joseph Lister at the Centennial International Exposition in Philadelphia later that year, it was my intent to portray the times as accurately as possible. Any success is due to scores of online and archival resources; any lapse is due to my imperfect interpretation.

Gravestone of John Wesley "Jack" Plummer, 1850–1912 (FindAGrave.com)

I'd like to once again thank the Ad Hoc Writers of Lubbock, Texas, who have provided sincere and diligent advice with each evolving chapter. The Crew of the Barque Lone Star, the Dallas-based scion society of the Baker Street Irregulars, welcomed me into their fold during pandemic-era virtual meetings, and allowed me a glimpse of their copious knowledge of, and assiduous dedication to, the works of the Master. The Caprock Writers & Illustrators Alliance, also of Lubbock, has bolstered this series with regional promotion. Tiffany Scofield, who took a chance on adding Will Brandon to the Five Star stable of Western authors with *The Wolf Hunt* in 2019, has been a smart and supportive editor.

About the Author

WILL BRANDON IS A PSEUDONYM for Barbara Brannon of Spur, Texas. In her work in preservation and tourism and throughout her career as writer and editor, she has dug deep into the history of the Lone Star State and traveled many miles of its highways and byways. Her history articles have appeared in the *Journal of the Wild West History Association, Authentic Texas* magazine, and *Lubbock Magazine,* and her Western-themed poems in *Weaving the Terrain: 100-Word Southwestern Poems* and *Bearing the Mask: Southwest Persona Poems.* She holds the M.A. and Ph.D. from the University of South Carolina, where she studied with novelist and poet James Dickey, and is coauthor, with Kay Ellington, of the Paragraph Ranch series of contemporary West Texas novels. WWW.BARBARABRANNON.COM

An amazing blend of mystery mixed with Western culture. Drama and
action compel the reader to turn the pages until the final satisfying end.
—HISTORICAL NOVELS REVIEW

When reverence for classic literature combines with excellent writing and
a knack for atmospheric description, the inevitable result is great reading.
Holmes and Watson themselves would approve—and so will you.
—JEFF GUINN, 2018 Western Writers of America Spur Award winner
for Best Traditional Novel

THE WOLF HUNT runs at the head of the pack as a great read.
— MIKE COX, author of *Gunsights and Sites in Texas Ranger History*

THE TALE OF 'THE WOLF HUNT'

Published in the anthology *Holmes and Me: Reflections on the World's Greatest Consulting*
Detective (July 2022) by the Crew and Passengers of The Barque Lone Star,
edited by Steve Mason and formatted by Liese Sherwood-Fabre

I HAVE BEEN ACCUSED BEFORE of "excellent pastiche." This, from
a laureate whose verse form I so admired that I wrote a response to his
call, and sent it to him; when his reply arrived with the above description
I fretted for weeks over whether I had committed a compliment or a crime.

I harbored similar misgivings about falling in with the long march of
re-visioners of Sherlock Holmes. Just who did I think I was, upstart crow of
a poet and editor, to lift the master's *Hound of the Baskervilles*—my favorite
Doyle tale since childhood—and plunk it down on the Texas frontier circa
1891? I wasn't a fiction writer. I harbored no extraordinary degree of fan
devotion. Hell, I wasn't even a true Texan, having earned my stripes during
a stint at a university press in Lubbock and learned my Lone Star history
by speed-reading *Texas,* Michener's doorstop of a novel, on the plane trip
there.

I'd like to think the inspiration was a brilliant and honorable one. That

I had first availed myself of the essential essays in *Beyond Baker Street,* or read the full canon, or delved more thoroughly into the storied tradition of Holmes homages before attempting my own.

But no, here I was one spring Saturday, out for a red-dirt ramble through a part of West Texas so sparsely populated it's been dubbed "The Big Empty," and noting the road's rugged twists and turns through dramatic canyon breaks. The setting sun glinted over a low-water crossing whose bottom looked uncertain for pickup or pack horse. The way back out defied the map; at dusk, at last, a fence line strung with the rotting pelts of unlucky coyotes gave onto the paved highway. This desolate landscape, I was certain, could match the moors chill for chill, and from that trip through the Croton Breaks sprang the vision of a creature chained there by an outlaw posing as a researcher, and the plight of his comely female relation.

I began "The Wolf Hunt" that night, hewing closely to the Hound by reworking portions of Doyle's original text. I read and reread the source to analyze plot twists, characterizations and clues, red herrings. I threw my late-night energies into a reimagined opening scene. I nicked a passage or two straight out of Doyle as a rap artist might sample glittering riffs from another song.

Spurred on by the positive feedback of my critique group, I persevered. Empowering Fort Worth consulting detective Derrick Miles to inveigle Doctor Frank Hooper into overseeing the death of rancher Basil Wolverton in remote Dickens County, I assembled scene upon scene. For a year I traveled nightly to that invented world, inviting into it episodes of my own creation and fictionalized figures of Texas history—and ornamenting it with a few more gems from the mother lode—until I had produced a full, original story that I hoped captured the Sherlockian spirit.

No embarrassment for this stepchild work led me to choose a pseudonym for publication when a paying contract was extended; on the contrary, I was quite proud of my counterfeit Hound, and opted to fly under the flag of male authorship only as a smart marketing strategy for the Western fiction category. Will Brandon's *The Wolf Hunt: A Tale of the Texas Badlands* appeared in April 2021, delayed six months thanks to Covid-19 bookstore and library closures, and took its place in the long progression of Sherlockian pastiche.

Also in a strategy of sincerest imitation, I had at my disposal a tool employed often by the Victorians: serialization in periodical form. As co-owner of a series of West Texas newspapers, I could bloody well run as many excerpts as the audience might bear—or at least as the publisher would permit.

Here, for the Crew of the Barque Lone Star's 5th anthology, I offer a portion of Chapter 1, "The Wide-Awake," with map and illustration (also sincere imitations) by the author.

Honorable tribute or shameful sham?

Reader, you be the judge.

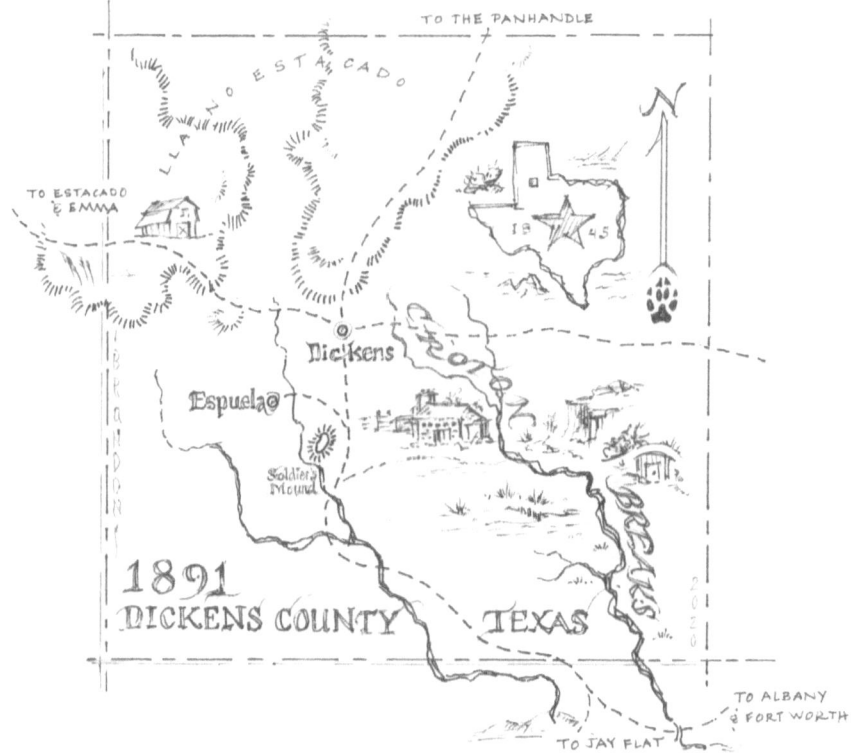

"BUT YOU HAVE FAILED TO NOTE ONE MATTER OF
SOME IMPORTANCE."

AN EXCERPT

from THE WOLF HUNT

Chapter 1
THE WIDE-AWAKE

{*In which Capt. Derrick Miles and Dr. Frank Hooper
discuss guns, hats, and boots.*}

IN THE FIFTEEN YEARS during which I have been acquainted with
Captain Derrick Miles, I have admitted him to be of a peculiar sort—prone
to bouts of profound meditation triggered by the partaking of tea extracted
from a certain cactus found in the Chihuahuan Desert, for instance, or excitable in the extreme when a moment of epiphany is visited upon him, say, in
the bathtub.

But nothing prepared me for the distressing sight that greeted me late on
a blustery autumn afternoon—the twelfth of October, I well recall—upon my
return to our shared bachelor quarters above the bootmaker's shop.

"Good God, man, don't do it!" I shouted instinctually and almost lunged
at him, before wiser caution caused me to step back. "Why don't you . . .
hand me . . . the gun?" I said in a more measured tone.

Derrick Miles, seated almost in profile to me at the teak-and-brass campaign desk as I stepped through the doorway, continued to hold the weapon
at arm's length with its barrel pointed toward the center of his face, which
appeared so thin in the shadows as to be almost cadaverous. He made no
move for several long seconds. I held my breath. He inched the muzzle closer
and squinted his eye toward it in the waning light.

"Miles, please—"

"Bring that lamp over here, would you, Hooper?"

I hesitated to shift my gaze from the scene, as though by my very force of will I might hold all the parts of it frozen and forestall disaster.

"That oil lamp, yes, please. And light it."

I abandoned my vigil for long enough to fetch the lamp. I slipped a friction match from the box on the table, cranked up the wick, and struck the match, keeping Miles in my sights. I lit the wick and moved closer, shining the glow on the firearm whose business end was situated a fingerbreadth from Miles's eyeball.

"Aha, I knew it!" he exclaimed, so suddenly I almost lost my grip on the lamp.

"Knew what?" I asked in relief, as he lowered the gun.

"A hardened residue of varnish impregnated with grains of black powder."

"As one might expect to find inside the barrel of a gun?"

"As one might expect to find inside the barrel of a gun that hasn't been fired in some months—or years."

"You had some concern on that score?"

"At least we know there's no chance our visitor was a Ranger."

Miles continued to dangle my duller intellect just out of reason's reach, a not infrequent circumstance in our exchanges. "We've had an unanticipated visit. Our caller, Hooper, does not appear to have been a Texas Ranger. And that is very good indeed, since, where there is a Ranger, there also is trouble."

"Ah, certainly." I struggled to keep up. "You had a caller while I was away at the hospital, but did not see him?" Had Derrick Miles benefited from even the slightest contact with any stranger, he would surely have swiftly deduced the man's occupation, birthplace, age, nationality, and more. Such were his estimable powers of detection.

Miles rose slowly from his seat and indicated the door through which I had come. "That is correct; I was out for the day as well, attending the mayor's meeting with members of the state Railroad Commission, about which I will enlighten you later. While you and I were gone a man lingered long enough in the upstairs corridor to have dropped crumbs from his biscuit. But he also left behind two valuable possessions. The gun—a six-chambered Colt revolver commonly known as the 'Peacemaker'—and this."

Still holding the gun, Miles stepped over to the hat rack beside the door.

From amid a row of pegs on which hung his favorite Boss-of-the-Plains Stetson, a plaid Scottish hunting cap he sometimes wore in adverse weather, an ancient and stained cavalry hat, and my own second-best black bowler, he lifted an old-fashioned, wide-brimmed sort seldom seen these days in Fort Worth, Texas.

I removed my preferred bowler from my head and rested it on the vacated peg, smoothing my hair back from my brow and brushing the dust from my moustache. I hung my overcoat, also dusty from the streetcar ride across town, on the hook beneath it. Miles motioned me to the velvet settee beside the hearth, where Mrs. Simpson's boy had set coals to burn in the grate. I welcomed the warmth after the shock I'd experienced at first seeing Miles with the gun.

"Take a look, Hooper," he said, turning the hat so I could inspect its inside. There I read, stamped in gold, "BOLLMAN | PHILADELPHIA | 1871."

"What do you deduce from this information?" he asked, standing with his back to me, hands clasped behind him.

"Our visitor was a gentleman and a Yankee?"

He turned to warm his other side. "Perhaps. One of sufficient age and thrift as to have held onto his hat for two decades, and to have preserved it all the way West. You might recall, as I do from an advertisement in an old issue of *Puck*, that the renowned haberdasher was established in sixty-eight. And something else."

I peered closely to examine the napless black felt of its manufacture, which appeared to me to be of superior quality but scuffed; the wide silk hatband, which was glossy but soiled; and the sweatband inside, where I noted a small paper label tucked in. "Six and seven-eighths! The owner must have a rather small head. Do you concur?"

"Indeed, my dear Hooper. You'll catch on yet. But you have failed to note one matter of some importance."

"I have?"

"Run your fingers across the crown, and lean in and use your olfactory sense as well. What do you detect?"

I did as instructed, and my fingers immediately picked up traces of dark particles, a whiff of which revealed the smell of—coal smoke. "The owner has arrived on the train—rather recently, I suppose."

"Precisely. You do my methods proud," said Miles, standing and proceed-ing to light the gas lamps beside the mantel as he spoke. "Have I ever told you how gratifying I find your studious attentiveness, and the faithfulness with which you record our deliberations? Some men, not necessarily radiat-ing light of their own, possess the rare gift of reflecting it from others, and some, while not generating waves of ideas themselves, excel at bouncing back an original sound, magnified and transformed. By Jove, Hooper, I see that quality in you. I am greatly in your debt."

He had seldom come so near to a compliment, and I must admit that his words gave me keen pleasure, for I had often been piqued by the indiffer-ence of Miles—five years my junior—to my admiration and to the continual attempts which I had made to spread the fame of his practice. I was proud, too, to think that I had so far mastered his approach as to apply it in a way which earned his approval. He now took the hat from my hands and examined it for a few minutes with his naked eyes. Then with an expression of interest he carried it to the window, where he looked over it again in the fading light with a convex lens.

"Interesting, though elementary," said he as he returned to his favorite corner of the settee. "There are certainly one or two indications upon the hat. It gives us the basis for several deductions."

"Has anything escaped me?" I asked with some self-importance. "I trust that there is nothing of consequence which I have overlooked?"

"I am afraid, my dear Hooper, that at least one of your conclusions may have been off the mark. When I said that you amplified my thinking I meant that in noting your fallacies I am often steered towards the truth. Not that you are entirely wrong in this instance. The man certainly hails, originally, from distant parts. But he may have spent more time on the frontier than is immediately evident. Do no theories suggest themselves? You know my teachings. Think!"

"I can think only of the obvious conclusion that the man must be at least somewhat absentminded."

He chuckled. "No flies on your hide, Hooper. But we can delve deeper. With what groups of wearers has such a hat customarily been associated?"

"Well, it puts me in mind of a certain country preacher I once knew, who rode the circuit in South Texas when I practiced in Galveston. A Methodist, I believe."

"Now, it's doubtful the owner of the hat is presently a minister here, don't you agree?—since you and I are aware of the clergy in all the churches of this city. What, then?" Miles strode to a tall cherry bookshelf from which he pulled a bound volume. He thumbed it until arriving at a certain page. "Eureka!—here we have it."

I cocked an eyebrow expectantly.

Miles intoned in singsong, "Of all the hats I ever see, / The wide-awake is the one for me: / 'Tis only truth when I declare, How it's the fashion everywhere!"

I waited, unenlightened, for more.

"A bit of doggerel published in *Notes and Queries,* volume 10, September 1872. Penned by one Stephen Jackson, Esquire, in 1859, as 'A New Song on an Old Hat,' to be sung to the tune of 'The Leathern Bottle.'"

Just for good measure, Miles lifted his violin from its stand and bowed a few notes. But the melody triggered no recognition on my part, and he set the instrument down again with a tone of resignation.

"The style of hat, my dear Hooper, is known as a wide-awake. It was first popularized by two groups during the era of Lincoln: one, his ideological partisans; another, members of the Society of Friends in England and elsewhere."

"The Quakers?"

Miles returned to reading the verse. "And what d'ye say to the huge broad-brim / That shades the Quaker starch'd and prim?" He snapped the book shut. "The poem goes on for some seven or eight stanzas of such. I'll spare you them. Now, Hooper, make your pick. Friend of Franklin and Penn, or adherent of Honest Abe?"

I shook my head, smiling, in amazement at his virtuoso performance. "Bravo, bravo. Your ability to connect disparate bits of information astonishes. Not to mention your recall of detail, worthy of Mr. Brady's photographic art itself."

"Which is it, then?"

"I'll have to venture . . . the latter choice, given the political discourse with which the papers are filled these days. Labor disputes. The Grange. Tariffs. Dealings with the Railroad Commission."

"Very well, then, let us test your theory." Miles picked up the hat again and handed it to me, along with the magnifying glass. The raised angle of his beaked nose and the pursed set of his lips sent the unmistakable message that I'd taken the wrong fork in the road. "What do you see?"

I peered through the glass at the black felt and ran my hand across the crown. "Mmmm . . . ouch!" Something small and sharp had pricked the tip of my right index finger.

"Mesquite thorn, no?"

I licked the blood from my fingertip. "That smarts." I continued my perusal, noting a frayed portion of the brim that appeared to have been, well, *chewed.* But before I could venture more, Miles strode abruptly to the mantel and leaned his elbow there thoughtfully.

"Now the prime question remains: why does a Philadelphia Quaker debark from a train on the Texas frontier, take pains to visit the office of a consulting detective, then depart again without leaving behind so much as a print of dirt from his shoe, but instead leaving his frayed hat on the bench, and underneath it his revolver? *That* is what we need to know."

"He was—in a hurry?"

"One might surmise."

"He was—indisposed, or distracted, or, God forbid, waylaid . . .?"

"Those are likewise possibilities. But let us consider that first principle of forensic science, which is—"

"Occam's Razor," I finished for him, having been schooled on the thesis upon various occasions. "Among numerous possibilities, the simplest is the likeliest."

"Very good. And, our lodgings being situated above the busy shop of a certain workman, and the visitor's arrival and departure leaving no evidence on the floorboards, what explanation might spring to mind?"

"Boots!" I cried, chastising myself that this point had eluded me. "The visitor was downstairs being fitted for a pair of boots."

"And perhaps still is. If he is fortunate, he will retrace his steps and recall where he laid his hat."

About that time I heard, outside the still-open hall door and below, a tap of leather on tongue and groove. Then another, and another. The taps approached with some hesitation, continuing upward. Miles moved his lips, counting the stairs silently. *Fourteen . . . fifteen, sixteen . . . seventeen.* He raised his fist and pantomimed in perfect time to the knock that came next.

I parroted Miles's words. "He will retrace his steps and recall—"

A voice called out. "Hallo? I say, greeting, sirs."

The man who peeked through the doorway was middle-aged, blond, of average height, though slim as far as I could surmise, underneath the long cloth coat he wore. His beard was trimmed in the Donegal style, of medium length, sans moustache. Hatless he was indeed, though not bootless. And behind him followed a small dog, which quickly trotted past its master into our quarters.

"Good evening," said Miles, rising, to the caller. "We were expecting you. And your canine companion, who is likely at this very minute fetching—"

"My hat!" cried the visitor. "I feared I might never recover it this time." The dog, a medium-sized mongrel, had gone directly over to retrieve its master's hat from the table beside the settee. The man leaned down to take the hat and pet the dog, and placed the hat again on his size-six-and-seven-eighths head. He looked quite pleased with himself for a moment, before snatching it off again. "Where are my manners?"

I went over to invite him in. "Not to worry. I am Doctor Frank Hooper, and this is my esteemed colleague, Captain Derrick Miles. Please, come in and tell us your name?"

The visitor set his hat atop his pate again for long enough to dip the front of its brim deferentially, then remove it once more. His speech was stilted and formal. "Wesley Barlow, of Estacado, Crosby County, Texas, two hundred eighty miles north and west of here as the crow flies."

Miles cast a skeptical glance my way. "Damn, that's bad!" he said, shaking his head.

The befuddled man blinked through his spectacles. "How's that?"

"Only for us, in our hypotheses. Crosby County, you say?"

"Yes, sir. And late of Philadelphia, Pennsylvania, and Zionsville, Indiana."

"Aha! And do we surmise correctly that you belong to a particular religious sect of that region?"

He nodded. "Unless that circumstance renders thee unable to assist in the matter I have come to discuss."

"Most assuredly not," said Miles, before asking our guest, "What does Reverend Wesley Barlow, man of the cloth, ask of Derrick Miles, specialist in crime detection? Do be seated, and apprise us!"

"Mister, sir, Mister—a humble clerk of the Society of Friends. And an attorney-at-law in said county."

"*Mister* Barlow, then. Hooper and I place ourselves humbly at your service, as well, if we find we may be of assistance," said Miles. "Before we delve deeper into your business, however, I believe there is one other item you may have left behind."

Mr. Barlow did not register the hint at first, then burst into exclamation. "The revolver! Thee did safeguard it, I hope?"

"Have no concern on that score. It lies on the table yonder. Unloaded, I might add."

Mr. Barlow seemed to shrink to even less of a bulk beneath the coat, as he exhaled. "I would prefer not to have carried a firearm under any circumstance, but—"

"Go on?"

"As it happens I required one for defense, and that is partly why I have come to seek thee out. But before I had the opportunity to find thee here, as I was seated there in the corridor, waiting outside thy chambers in hopes of thy return, I heard footsteps approaching, starting up the stairs, and I—I hid the gun on the bench beneath my hat."

"You didn't wish, as a man of peace, to be mistaken for a desperado?"

"Something like that. The footsteps came no farther, and I retreated into the shadow of the corner."

"Heavens, man!" I cried. "Were you being pursued?"

"Not exactly . . . it's simply that I had not gone abroad in such a metropolis, nor in such a vicinity of evil, in many years, and after what has transpired in recent days I must have acted out of an overabundance of caution."

"And these—recent events gave you cause for fear?" asked Miles.

"Quite so. I traveled a full day and night by coach and then a day by train to bear witness of some extremely distressing occurrences in our region. Along the coach route our party of four—plus the driver and his guard—were beset by threat of beast and, at the very end, disembarking from the train compartment here at the very outskirts of the city only blocks from thy door, I encountered crime and vice of a most venial sort. After I alighted from the arduous journey at nearly dawn and proceeded on foot to my hotel, a blackguard leapt from the shadows and demanded money. I was able to satisfy him with a few coins from my pocket, my purse being well hidden, but as I withdrew I was accosted from another direction by a—a—"

"A grifter? A cutpurse?" I offered.

"I hesitate to say it. A woman of—eh, easy virtue."

Miles suppressed a smile. "Hell's Half-Acre," he said. "I must apologize on behalf of our adopted city. Fort Worth has become the standard-bearer for unsavory activity, I'm afraid—what with all manner of cowpunchers, carpetbaggers, and camp followers coming and going, with often questionable motives. I hope you weren't worse harmed."

"No, God be praised, except for thoroughly ruining my footwear as I ran senseless for blocks in search of a gentler quarter. I felt compelled to arm myself at the first opportunity, however. I went straightaway to Fowler's pawn shop and purchased the piece at second hand, then sought out a cobbler to repair my boots. I had no idea I'd landed literally at thy doorstep when I left them with Lewis downstairs."

"That makes two matters about which I have been correct, at least," said Miles.

"What are those?" I inquired.

"That there's truly no more useful site for a detective's office than upstairs from one of the first places any newcomer will go upon arriving in the city—the bootblack's—and that any man who leaves his gun behind on a bench isn't accustomed to shooting for a living."

Barlow let out a sigh. "Thee is most true on the latter statement. In my law practice I have specialized in land transactions, contracts, wills, that sort of thing. Nothing that would typically bring me into contact with the criminal element."

Miles went over and picked up the man's gun, and handed it butt-first to its owner. "Your next task might be to acquire a holster," he said. "And to clean your Colt thoroughly before you insert it." He then returned five bullets into the man's palm.

I stepped in to smooth over the awkward moment. "Might I offer us all some nourishment?" I took the opportunity to suggest. "You must be ravenous, Mr. Barlow, if you've had no meal or rest since morning."

"I slept away most of the day at the hotel," he admitted. "And thee is right, I would be most thankful for a morsel. I've had nothing other than the dry biscuits I brought with me from the train."

The dog, as though sensing the mention of food, perked up its ears.

Though it was nearly the dinner hour and the wind was still blowing mercilessly outside our windows, I lifted the telephone receiver on the side table and called downstairs for Mrs. Simpson, who grudgingly agreed to send her boy around to fetch a tray of sandwiches for us from the saloon. We were not at a loss for libations, as Miles and I customarily kept a goodly selection of whiskies and ports on hand. Mr. Barlow refused any, accepting only water.

Miles settled into the armchair near our guest and sipped his Jameson's, neat. "Let us learn more about the recent events you mentioned, Mr. Barlow."

"Yes, right. I came to thee, Derrick Miles, because I recognized that I am myself a simple man but now faced with a most serious and extraordinary problem. Recognizing, as I do, that thee is the second highest expert in the West—"

"Indeed, sir! May I inquire who has the honor to be the first?" asked Miles with some asperity.

"For strictly practical and business matters the work of the Pinkertons must always appeal strongly."

"Then had you not better consult them?"

"I said, sir, to the precisely practical mind. But in matters of solving great mysteries it is acknowledged that Derrick Miles stands alone. I trust, sir, that I have not inadvertently—"

"Just a little," said Miles. "I think, Mr. Barlow, you ought to just get down to business and tell me plainly the exact nature of your problem."

The wind, at that moment, whipped the downstairs door shut as Jake the servant boy trudged up the seventeen stairs with our supper. The dog twitched its ears in interest but did not move from its spot. We fell to our repast as Mr. Barlow laid open the case.

Available at online bookstores or via the author

BRONZE MEDAL, WILL ROGERS MEDALLION AWARD, 2021

FINALIST, WESTERN FICTIONEERS AWARD, 2021

THE WOLF HUNT
A Tale of the Texas Badlands
DERRICK MILES MYSTERIES, BOOK I

IN THE RUGGED, DESOLATE CROTON BREAKS OF WEST TEXAS a spectral creature with a six-inch pawprint has spooked livestock of late. When British-born cattle baron Basil Wolverton is found dead outside his own ranch gate, cowhands and nesters alike whisper of an ancestral curse, the dire wolf of legend.

Sir Basil's executor Wesley Barlow knows what he must do: catch the next train for Fort Worth, where consulting detective Derrick Miles and his assistant Doctor Frank Hooper are his best bet to figure out whether there's been a crime committed . . . or some diabolical force at work.

If the story sounds familiar, it should. Transporting the Sherlock Holmes classic *The Hound of the Baskervilles* to Dickens County, circa 1891, author Will Brandon reimagines Sir Arthur Conan Doyle's thrilling tale with a Texas twist on a murderous beast, a fugitive outlaw, greed and grit, affairs of the heart, and a landscape yet untamed.

In the heyday of Charles Goodnight and Quanah Parker—and one of the craftiest stalkers on the frontier—The Wolf Hunt traces Hooper's solemn pledge to solve the vexing case with which Miles has entrusted him and protect the Wolverton heir in his charge. But will bullets and iron bars bear out against the embodiment of evil? In this high Victorian adventure, the answer is anything but elementary.

COMING SOON

THE CASTLE OF FEAR
DERRICK MILES MYSTERIES, BOOK 3

———

AN EXCERPT

THE EMPTY CASTLE

Published in an anthology (forthcoming 2024) by the Crew and Passengers
of The Barque Lone Star, edited by Steve Mason
and formatted by Liese Sherwood-Fabre

SOME THREE YEARS AFTER the West Texas wolf scare during which
the entirely fictional Captain Derrick Miles and Doctor Frank Hooper
solved the entirely fictional case of Sir Basil Wolverton's unfortunate
demise, consulting detective Miles returns—apparently from the grave—on
a mission to track down the elusive con man and apparent serial murderer
Dr. H. H. Holmes.

The true-life crimes of Holmes (yes, the pseudonym was his twisted
and deliberate choice), born Herman Webster Mudgett in 1861, spanned
two decades in the 1880s and '90s across America and famously centered
on the "Murder Castle" he built in Chicago to serve patrons of the 1893
World's Columbian Exposition. Accounts of his perverse mind and nefar-
ious deeds have been widely recorded and even more widely speculated
upon; one of the best-known novelizations was Erik Larson's 2003 *The
Devil in the White City,* which refreshed for modern-day readers Holmes's
international infamy dating back to the "yellow journalism" era of the
1890s.

What fewer fans of crime and suspense know is that H. H. Holmes, only months before his 1894 arrest, also constructed a "Murder Castle" in the heart of Fort Worth, Texas. Yes, this is verifiably true—as is the Texas-based charge of horse theft against Holmes, which played a significant part in his ultimate downfall.

Given the previously determined choice of Fort Worth as the detective duo's London in the award-winning pastiche *The Wolf Hunt: A Tale of the Texas Badlands* (2021), the story of the city's real-life Murder Castle begged to be retold as a sequel.

The standalone segment below is adapted from a novel in progress titled "The Castle of Fear." While it necessarily fictionalizes some circumstances—let alone riffs freely upon the master's canonical tales "The Empty House," and "Silver Blaze"—care has been taken to research and preserve tantalizing factual details as well as the local and world events and places within which the story has been set.

Return with me, then, to the Panther City, as it begins to emerge from its outpost cowtown roots. Cattle shipping on a tarantula-shaped network of railroads has led Fort Worth to boom; multi-story brick business houses are quickly replacing rough-and-ready board buildings; sidewalks are being laid; telephone exchanges and bicycles are facts of daily life; an imposing pink-granite courthouse is rising on the bluffs above the Trinity River. Famed city marshal "Longhair Jim" Courtright has already been dispatched to his grave by Luke Short, and the Sundance Kid has yet to arrive; oil has been struck in the region; Hell's Half Acre thrives; and there are fortunes to be made. It's anybody's guess whose they might be.

—*Barbara Brannon, Crew of the Barque Lone Star, September 2023*

DERRICK MILES WAS DEAD.

And had been for precisely two years and seven months to the day, a fact I knew from my own witness but could still hardly fathom. I had seen with my very eyes the unsurvivable fall from a great height, Miles and his foeman plunging into the deep gorge at the Pecos High Bridge. The ocular proof had been incontrovertible, the disappearance of the world's first and foremost consulting detective attested to by myself and accepted by all.

Yet here he was in the flesh, on the last afternoon of October in the year of our Lord 1894, striding a half step ahead of me along Fort Worth's bustling Main Street, as had so often been our custom on shared missions of yore. In the stained duster, spurs, and much-used Stetson he'd acquired moments ago from a secondhand dealer in men's furnishings, he dodged recognition, as did I in similar disguise.

The fog had burned away, pushed aside by a fitful wind, by the time we turned the corner east onto Fifth.

"We're not going back to the apartment?" I asked.

"Not for the moment," replied Miles. "It's surely being watched. We'll do well to keep our partnership under wraps—quite literally—for the time being. Nicetameetcha, Al—I'm Zeb." We knotted our scarves nearly to our ears. I shouldn't have worried. North on Rusk, we fell right in with the assorted pedestrians—busy clerks, bustle-bottomed ladies with skirts aflutter and maids and children in tow, delivery boys with wheeled carts throwing up trails of dust, bandanaed cowhands like ourselves—hoofing it north toward the courthouse or south toward the stockyards or every which way to all manner of emporiums and eateries, for Fort Worth seemed to have blossomed into a more modern and, dare I say, respectable, place even during my hermitage. I gazed in awe as a tall, two-wheeled contraption lunkered by, almost grazing my elbow as its rider pedaled laboriously uphill. The bicycle craze, I had to admit, held no fascination for me.

From his rucksack my pardner Zeb retrieved a lariat and casually practiced tricks as we walked, dropping the loop over hitching posts as we strolled up the hill. The rope, made of a dark, glistening fiber wound with an outer layer like a piano string, appeared unusually supple. I wondered where he'd acquired it—or his skill in using it—but I asked no questions.

At the corner of Fourth, where a uniformed patrolman directed vehicle and pedestrian traffic by means of whistle and gloved hands, we waited our turn to cross. I let my eye rest upon the familiar brick exterior of the Fort Worth Land Title building, cater-cornered to us, where in previous days Miles and I had frequently consulted records; then allowed it to travel up the block to the handsome, four-story façade of the Natatorium. I had often recommended to my patients the health benefits of its Turkish baths and indoor swimming pool, from my firsthand knowledge as a founding patron.

Farther along, the opera house had once also been a favorite haunt of mine—and of Miles as well, before his unexplained hiatus. In this familiar but foreign-feeling scene I spied no sign of awareness on the faces around me that the great detective was once again in their midst.

The patrolman's whistle signaled, and we joined the throngs crossing Fourth Street. "Well, here we are, Al," said the detective, hooking his thumb toward a hot-food wagon at the corner. The aroma of sizzling steak wafted our way. I realized he was talking to me. "Whaddya say, let's grab a bite?" he added in with a twang. "Ah'm *hon*-gry!"

Cowboy Zeb strode over, fished into his pocket for a quarter, and returned with a portable meal wrapped in waxed paper for each of us. Like the other workingmen, we found a perch at the edge of the plank sidewalk, folded back the wrapper, and tucked in. The luncheon sandwich turned out to be a grilled patty made from shredded beef laid between slices of bread, and dressed with pickles and Heinz mustard. And it was—delicious.

"Hamburger, they call it," said Zeb. "Now, let's git down to business. Up the street—what do you see?" He cocked his head in that direction, where I spotted, to my astonishment, a forbidding-looking, three-story brownstone pile in progress—that had not existed the last time I'd set foot here.

"Our destination," he explained between bites.

"But I didn't even know about this . . . what is it?"

"I realize you haven't been out and about. But you must not have been reading the papers, either."

"No," I admitted.

"It is, to all accounts, a boardinghouse—of a hundred rooms, it's said. Not all of 'em with doors."

A shiver tickled my spine. Puzzlement must have shown on my face, for my companion went on.

"This is what brought me back from the netherworld, though I did not know it at the time. And I have begun to suspect it is its own brand of hell." He paused to let that sink in, and I gulped down the last bite of my Hamburger sandwich. "They call it the Castle."

"Who is building it?"

"Ah, my friend, that is the question, isn't it? Come, let us take an obser-vational tour."

Zeb reached into the pocket of his duster for a pouch of chewing tobacco and inserted a plug into his cheek, a finishing touch to his ruse. We crossed Rusk back to the other side, where the three- and four-story buildings shielded us somewhat from the gusting north wind.

"What grabs you first, Al?"

I glanced up surreptitiously to avoid notice as we slowed to a shuffle. "Well, that shore is a heap of brickbats, Zeb," I replied. I thought I detected a chuckle beneath Zeb's face covering, in response to my attempt at charade.

"All o' that done got throwed up in less time'n it'd a took fer a passel of armadillo pups to git borned," said my partner. Miles stepped closer and snapped out of character. "Word around town is, work crews changed out every few days. Tradesmen got fired with no notice, new ones came in to take up where those left off."

"I—I never even noticed," I replied. If Miles had a clue why I hadn't, he didn't let on.

He continued with his forensics. "Talk in some corners of City Hall is that the builder, one Benton T. Lyman, was playing a shell game with his contractors. He and his business associate, a Mr. Pratt, would use a parcel of land as collateral to obtain materials. Once a workman finished a portion and looked to get paid, they'd find some minor fault with it, put him off. The furnishings and fixtures they'd also bought on credit, they'd turn around and hock for cash, which they then used to string the crews along, just enough to stave off a suit."

"Well, surely if work has come to a standstill and folks are onto their scheme, these men will now be brought to account?"

"There also seems to be some confusion of identities," he said. "No one is really sure who Pratt and Lyman are . . . and I for one have a theory that 'Lyman' carries an ironic double meaning."

I rubbed my chin, considering this, as I gazed up at the brick trim of the unfinished third story.

"Back in July, it appears, the partners may have skipped town, together or separately. Or it's possible either or both have been right in our midst, masked among the masses as convincingly as you and I."

I cast a glance over my shoulder, measuring the aspects of the random faces passing us on the sidewalk, neither man nor woman nor child giving any hint of recognition to a duo who, a relatively short time ago, were as well known as any in the city. It was equally surprising to me that I had, so far, encountered not a soul *I* knew. Yes, Miles was right. Fort Worth had become busy and crowded enough to hide a criminal of any stripe who determined not to be found. I felt a frisson, a hint of winter rawness to come.

Turning my gaze upward, I asked my companion, "What about that turret on the corner? Seems out of character . . . the rest of the building is just a big flat ugly box with shuttered windows."

"'S'all rather haphazard, ain't it, Al?" he replied, pausing to spit a chunk of tobacco on the sidewalk and then cocking his head for me to resume our pace. "See that there shop directly below it on the ground floor?"

"Yup," I nodded.

"At's a 'pothecary shop in the makin'. Might be the owner deals in some patent medicines and the like, y'know. Might be he wants to keep an eye on comin's and goin's down both streets, too, if ya see what I mean." He turned his chin upward and shielded his eyes against the dust.

"Yep, I do, Zeb. Yep, I reckon yore right. It ain't the most elegant arky-tekcher for sech a tony quarter, either, if y'ask me."

"You speak the God's truth, Al. Almost like th' owners didn't want it to git noticed on the front page of the papers." We walked slowly west on Second, stealing glances at the structure. I marveled at its proximity to our own digs. *Former* digs, I reminded myself. This monstrosity would have cast a morning shadow over the stretch of Main Street behind our own apartments at 221B Houston.

"I got one question fer ya, Zeb," I uttered, leaning closer and pausing to pull down my kerchief as the wind and dust battered my face full on. "Where's th'other winders and doors?"

"I 'speck hotel guests might be wonderin' that too. This place ain't likely to git many bookin's if the tourists cain't enjoy a view of the river or a eyeful of that brand-new courthouse goin' up."

Miles was right. Anyone lodging on the third floor might expect to be rewarded with a northward vista across the Trinity bluffs, with a front-row seat to the construction of the imposing Renaissance Revival granite landmark rising on the hilltop. Even now I spied, above the parapets of Second Street, a dozen workers clambering across the scaffolding around the courthouse's center tower, and could hear the echo of their chisels and hammers ringing through the alleyway. Yet nowhere on this side of the Castle was any glazing in evidence. Window apertures were instead boarded up and painted the same dun brown as the stone, and even in the middle of the block where one might have expected a side door for the public, the entrance space was bricked over. There was no fire escape.

At the alley, I followed Miles's gaze to the left. Stacks of building materials lined the dirt passageway, leaving room only wide enough for the rubbish cart to pass. Again, no doorway, no ladder.

Unaccustomed as I had grown to outdoor exercise, I felt a weariness settle into my bones, along with a hearty distaste for this blemish on the city's skyline. "I'm bushed, Zeb," I said, stepping back into my stage role. "Kin we stop in fer a sodey pop?"

"We're outta luck here, pardner. Place never even opened for bidness. Boarded up tighter'n a banker's fist. But don'tchew worry, I got a plan for gittin' us inside. It'll be comin' on dark here in a bit. Let's go have us a jigger of somethin' stronger than sodey while we wait."

I hiked up my galluses and pulled my duster tighter around my shoulders. It was beginning to look like we were in for a night of it.

At a saloon on Weatherford where we'd once been regulars, we took a back-corner table as Zeb and Al. The young bartender greeted us with a "What'll it be, strangers?" and soon returned with a brace of Lone Star pints. The beer went down smooth and delicious, and I ventured to ask Miles if he'd missed our favorite local brew during his, ah, absence.

"Glad as I am to be back on Texas soil," he replied cannily, "it cannot hold a candle to a Truman's East End porter, my friend."

"You were—you've been—in *London?*"

He smiled wryly. "You're disappointed that I bring no report from the pearly gates—or those of Hades," he said.

I nodded. "You owe me some explanation, don't you think?"

Miles shifted his chair around where he could keep a better eye on the front door and pulled his hat down at an angle. He lowered his voice and abandoned the drawl. "What I'm about to tell you bears on one of the most horrendous chapters in the world's criminal history, and delves into the darkest recesses of a fiend's deviant mentality. Yet I promise you, the investigation in which I have been involved was in no way premeditated. It was an opportunity dropped in my lap, Hooper. One I could not pass up."

I motioned for another round. "I for one have had enough of this soul-ing-and-guising for one Hallow's Eve," I said. "It's time for the truth." We settled in as the afternoon shadows deepened.

"Let us begin at the Pecos River," he said in a tone not much more than a whisper. "On a bright March morning with a railroad president aboard a train."

"I've not forgotten."

"I was not expecting Professor MacHinery himself to also be aboard," Miles continued. "I thought his attack would come from below and from the rim of the gorge, where his minions, as we know, were already in place. But I was prepared for an array of possibilities. With this." He pulled back the edge of his duster to reveal a glimpse of the black lariat.

"Go on."

"You've seen the versatility of this rope. It is my own invention, employ-ing rubber harvested from the Amazon jungles and reinforced with a thin cable of steel. It is capable of supporting the weight of a man—or two—and stretching to twice its length before springing back. I call it *bom-jebe*."

He laid the slack end of it across the table as an invitation for me to check his claim. I found the rope supple and strong, and I was able with some exertion to extend a short section even as he had described.

"The one I had brought with me aboard the Union Pacific train that day saved my life even as MacHinery plummeted onto the rocks beneath the channel of the Pecos. As the villain pushed me from the platform of the train I managed to wrest myself loose and catch this end"—he revealed a mighty iron hook that had been hidden in the cable—"on the trestle. Three successively shorter—and terrifying—bounces of the line left me hanging halfway above the water and able, in due time, to haul myself back up. You, and the train, were long gone. If any of MacHinery's henchmen witnessed my survival, they had scattered; but after a few days, when I heard no word to controvert that of my apparent demise, I saw my chance. A week later, after I'd crossed into Mexico and walked for seven nights across the Pensamiento, I was able to send a coded message from the Allende village to my brother Percy in London."

"You telegraphed him rather than me . . . " I trailed off. "Why did you not at least let me know?"

"You couldn't have kept the secret, amigo. The genuineness of your mourning—witnessed by our enemies as well as our allies—was the most convincing evidence in all quarters that I had not survived. Don't you see: the members of MacHinery's mob got over their own grief so quickly, they quarreled among themselves and grew cocky. Many were easy marks for arrest all around the world. Some surrendered; some were imprisoned; some hanged. You read of this in the papers, I trust?"

"No. I read nothing. I struggled to put one foot in front of the other, to tend to a few patients . . . until I became one myself."

Miles paused at this, then nodded slowly before continuing. "We had our informants, of course. We knew you had vacated 221B." He paused again as though waiting for acknowledgment—or forgiveness. He took out his pipe, filled it, lit it, and drew on it, before resuming his narrative. "Well then. Here you are, and glad I am of it."

"You left off in Coahuila," I prompted. "Go on."

"Yes, Coahuila. From there I made my way by train to San Antonio and New York, then sailed for England. All undercover, though the passage was not without its tense moments. By May Day I was sitting in my brother's office at the ministry to hear him out on a secret mission. Percy can be quite persuasive, as you know. He convinced me that a ghost might prove the best man for the job of tracking a killer."

"You mentioned the name, this morning, of Jack the Ripper. The Whitechapel murderer. Did you have any success?"

Miles took another long draw on his meerschaum, then puffed the smoke out in a series of little rings. Two more beers arrived. He leaned in closer and drew his scarf up around his ears as the afternoon shadows deepened.

"Imagine with me, if you will, an ordinary day at the city's Diogenes Club, which I myself can only imagine, as I was not present, having kept carefully out of public view for two and a half years. I picture the setting thus. My elder half-brother, dapper in his customary afternoon sack suit and starched collar, is occupying his customary leather chair beside his customary smoking stand while in his hand is his customary gin and tonic with lime. Customarily, Percival Miles would be deep in thought, holding court with his own company.

"But in strides a stranger. A Yankee, and not just any American, but a

true Boston barney, a preceptor of drama at a Back Bay school of performing arts. This much and more Percy learns after the stranger takes a seat
opposite him while he sips his own beverage, clearly not his first of the day.
The gent is a member of a reciprocating club, the Lambs, and has been
on the continent and in England for a fortnight, taking in a few shows and
seeing museums; it is his chief aim, however, to trace the whereabouts of
a onetime ward and student of his, an orphaned female cousin who had
fallen out of communication with her remaining kin soon after becoming
engaged to marry in Chicago.

"Percy continues to listen, saying little as the visitor eases deeper into his
cups. A handful of letters from the young woman discussing vague plans to
travel abroad with her new husband are all he has had to go on. Said husband, it seems, has a questionable past. Some months on, the Pinkertons
have been consulted, but their man has turned up nothing useful. For a
year now, the stranger says, he has been carrying around a gnawing feeling
that something might be very wrong, as the young lady had fully intended
to return to a budding career as a stage presenter and elocution teacher.

"Percy, not typically one to suffer anyone's random ramblings, catches
a few words that pique his interest. The missing woman, says the visitor,
has inherited valuable property—land and cash and horses—in Fort Worth,
Texas."

My eyes opened wide, my sudden gaze momentarily breaking the plane
of Miles's little drama.

"Yes, Hooper, you've heard me right. 'Minnie had every expectation
of going back after her summer at the Chicago fair,' says the man. 'She
would never have abandoned her dreams, or her younger siblings. And
then Nannie the quiet one didn't write back either....'

"Bear with me just a little longer in this narrative, the import of which
you may begin to grasp. It is the visitor's last day abroad before returning
home with nothing, he tells Percy. If only he knew someone with better
connections . . . Percy asks for the man's card, accepts it, rises slowly,
instructs him to wait, walks casually to the club's telephone office, places a
call to a secret number. Professor Fred Williams of Boston, Massachusetts,
does not realize that he has poured out his drunken soul to the one man in
all London with precisely the right resources to assist."

I took this all in. Miles had painted a picture so vivid I expected to glance up and find myself surrounded by the stuffed shirts and cigar smoke of the Diogenes, and to observe Percival Miles himself returning to his chair. "Your brother sensed a correlation with the larger thread of unsolved crimes you'd been pursuing," I said.

"Enough to suggest that the time was ripe to act. Despite everything we'd painstakingly pieced together, the Whitechapel killer remained unknown—and quite possibly at large. One theory I myself had begun to advance led—and still leads—to an American perpetrator, one with a skewed mentality regarding women, a keen understanding of human anatomy, some skill with a knife, and an extraordinary talent for disguise and misdirection."

"Not unlike yourself," I interjected coolly, baiting him.

"You jest, but the gift of virtually inhabiting the criminal mind carries its advantages. I had spent my hiatus doing precisely that *sub rosa*, reenacting scenes, examining evidence, following every strand of speculation in the Ripper cases—as well as many facts unknown to the rank and file—thanks to Percy's access. Together he and I had systematically eliminated all known suspects put forth over the years by Scotland Yard. Strange as it might seem, the picture had begun to emerge of a U.S. citizen, male, white, born sometime before the war—possibly the fifties—with submissive mother, domineering father, taunting siblings; and possibly a wife of his own and child, or children, by now. Our man claims a degree of medical training. Though he is not traditionally handsome, he also possesses a portion of charm; in physique he is of average height and weight, with no distinguishing features other than ample facial hair—brown. He is sufficiently vain about his appearance, however, that he generally wears mutton chops, as well as a bowler to cover his receding hairline or, perhaps, baldness."

At this I cast a glance up at him.

"No personal offense intended, of course. Now, where were we . . . . He is not wealthy. Though probably not gainfully employed in a particular job, he is clever at obtaining anything on credit and has amassed sufficient means to parlay small sums into larger schemes. His victims are always vulnerable, even gullible. He is a frequent, and erratic, traveler by train. He is a voracious reader of newspapers. He holds a savant's fascination with clues and ciphers. It was this latest characteristic I had landed upon, Hooper, only the week before Doctor Williams's chance encounter with

Percy at the Diogenes Club. My casual source at Hatchards—on my under-cover rounds I had taken to scouting not only the Paternoster stalls but the established bookshops—fell to discussing the escalating fascination with the detective stories of Arthur Conan Doyle. I recall that you yourself were an early adherent?"

I nodded assent.

"'The author's stories in The Strand have suddenly become the store's hottest seller,' the man said. 'Imagine that, eclipsing Dickens and Stevenson and even the Bard . . . this upstart writer for the masses!' and such. He prac-tically sniffed the air as he recalled his first fanatical customer, back in '87. A New England traveler had stopped in to specifically request the *Beeton's Christmas Annual* for that season. This might not have been a memorable occasion, of course, but the man appeared so taken with his find when the clerk handed it to him, he stood right there at the register and devoured the entire cover story—and then had to be reminded as he started to walk off without paying. 'Shall I take down your name, sir, in order to notify you when future works by this author arrive?' the clerk asked him. 'Yes, by all means,' he answered. 'You may find me via a notice in the papers to Doctor Henry—ah, Doctor H. H. Holmes.'"

I mulled the possible repercussions of Miles's narrative as I found myself drawn inexorably into this caliginous London landscape. To think that the most notorious killer of our age might have been a citizen of our own advanced shores—and not some escapee from Bedlam or aberrant throw-back to the Picts—cast the Whitechapel murders in a different frame of reference indeed. What would have possessed an American to abandon the privileges of our thriving democracy and go in search of victims abroad? Perhaps the man was widely known, or perhaps widely enough known in certain circles . . . perhaps he intended to hone his skill, and return . . .

I did not realize that I was speaking these theories aloud until Miles leaned toward me and interrupted.

"Precisely, Hooper," he said. "I had already come to the conclusion that the killer had planned to rehearse, to exercise his technique; most likely, on female victims he deemed expendable. He bore no moral prejudice toward the class of Englishwoman he targeted; he simply guessed that fewer ener-gies would be put forward in pursuing a perpetrator. On this score he was wrong. The whole of Scotland Yard devoted years to the effort, under the likes of Abberline, Moore, and Andrews. Detective Inspector McWilliam himself got in on the action. But ultimately their work was as inconclusive as that of your Lestrade and Gregson in those potboilers you're so fond of."

"Did you yourself make more progress during your sojourn?" I asked, trying to maintain a casual tone.

"No, frankly, not in the sort of proof the Metropolitan Police were looking for—eager as they were to remove the stain of embarrassment resulting from a notoriously unsolved murder discovered right on their own premises."

"You refer to the woman's dismembered body found in Whitehall in the fall of '88," I offered.

"Indeed. The police believed that incident unconnected to the so-called Ripper cases," he said nonchalantly. "They were—and are—quite wrong. Once the trail of evidence in Great Britain grew cold, around '91, the London police abandoned the chase, and the matter has been allowed to stand as a mystery in the public's imagination. Percy's chance visitor provided the missing link for me."

"How so?"

"Fred Williams said that his niece's mystery suitor—later husband, though an unlawful one, I'm certain—claimed to be a medical doctor." I raised an eyebrow at this revelation. "You are no doubt aware, my dear physician, of the inconsistent nature of standards and licensure in the profession in the 1880s."

"Despite Doctor Osler's vigorous campaigning, of course," I added. "The situation is only now beginning to turn about."

"Eighty thousand self-described doctors in the United States—according to our most recent Census tally—and no consistent, nationwide registry by which to verify their credentials. And the medical schools themselves have only of late started to professionalize. It was, and still is, far easier for someone falsely claiming to be a medical practitioner in our nation to elude discovery than in the mother country. A clever forger with a nimble hand could move about at will, peddle snake-oil, cure a few ills, perform easy procedures, and fool many. Once I had a name to go by—and a fortnight's access to Fred Williams' correspondence and recollections as I accompanied him back home under cover—I was able to pick up that faint trail left by our Doctor H. H. Holmes from Whitechapel westward across the ocean to Boston, then on to Chicago, St. Louis, Denver, and here. At every stop I learned something useful, and a picture began to emerge."

The light was fast fading, and a distinct chill was descending, by the time Miles brought his narrative to a close. "Our killer was known in New England as Mudgett, in Chicago as Holmes and later Gordon, in Denver as Howard, and most recently, in Fort Worth, as Pratt or Bond. The most diligent and painstaking work has been required to prove beyond doubt that these figures are one and the same."

"How marvelous! And will you arrest him?"

"That final task, I would prefer, as was my former custom, to leave to the local authorities. But there's only one main complication at this point."

"What would that be?"

"Our Mr. Lyman the investor has slipped the dragnet again."

"He's left Fort Worth?"

"I sent Agent Nicholls northward after him," said Miles. "For now, our concern is with the fake doctor Holmes himself. We must find a way into his murder castle—and to prevent him from repeating his previous atrocities on Texas soil." He indicated with a nod over his shoulder that we should pay up and be on our way. The Hallow's Eve goblins would soon roam abroad, eager to practice their pranks; bicycles and storefronts were padlocked, shoppers were long since scattered to the warmth of their parlors, and Derrick Miles was itching with a theory to test.

Night was falling, and I gathered that its shadows would supply ample cover for whatever the resurrected detective next had in mind.

READERS MIGHT ALSO ENJOY

Book One
The Paragraph Ranch

Kay Ellington & Barbara Brannon

Every writer knows you can't go home again. But that's just what is required of West Texas expatriate Dee Bennett-Kaufmann when her mother is badly injured in a mysterious car accident. Single-again "Dr. Dee" has never been on the "A-team" in her trendy East Coast MFA program. When a prestigious summer fellowship gives her the chance to finally finish her book, salvage her career, and spend some quality time with her college-age daughter — Dee's certain her luck is about to change. Returning to care for her irascible, widowed mother threatens all of that. With so much at stake, Dee engineers a series of unorthodox strategies and creative tradeoffs to keep her options in play—and despite herself finds friendship, love, and the power of words in the unlikeliest of places.

Give a Cup of Water
A Paragraph Ranch Tale

Barbara Brannon

The citizens of Claxton, Texas, are justifiably possessed with a healthy thirst — on the dusty plains of West Texas, they're in the midst of a seven-year drought when the town finally votes to go wet. The opposition faction, and its leader, Miss Jessica Cater, manage to shut down the promotion beer-store owner Buck Turlock has cooked up just in time for the Fourth of July celebration. But will Buck's schemes lead Miss Jessie to rethink her position?